ASTRONAUT!

Also by Oana Aristide:

UNDER THE BLUE

ASTRONAUT!

Oana Aristide

WILDFIRE

First published in Trade Paperback in 2026 by Wildfire
An imprint of Headline Publishing Group Limited

1

Cataloguing in Publication Data is available from the British Library

Trade Paperback ISBN 978 1 0354 2082 7

Typeset in Dante MT by CC Book Production
Printed and bound in Great Britain by Clays Ltd, Elcograf S.p.A.

MIX
Paper | Supporting
responsible forestry
FSC® C104740

Headline's policy is to use papers that are natural, renewable and
recyclable products and made from wood grown in well-managed forests
and other controlled sources. The logging and manufacturing processes are
expected to conform to the environmental regulations of the country of origin.

HEADLINE PUBLISHING GROUP
An Hachette UK Company
Carmelite House
50 Victoria Embankment
London EC4Y 0DZ

The authorised representative in the EEA is Hachette Ireland,
8 Castlecourt Centre, Dublin 15, D15 XTP3, Ireland
(email: info@hbgi.ie)

www.headline.co.uk
www.hachette.co.uk

To John Petherbridge and Laurence Van Der Noordaa

If it is not right do not do it; if it is not true do not say it.

Marcus Aurelius, *Meditations*

1

Sighişoara, March

Lia is being walked home by Comrade Blaga, the shopkeeper, who is holding her hand. A couple of times she tries to get out of this embarrassing situation, makes her hand go limp, or folds it together in the shape of a small bird wriggling out of a nest. But Comrade Blaga does not let small birds go.

They are walking by the road along the river embankment. It's Mother's birthday and also Friday afternoon, and the buses are bringing people home from the factories. From the corner of her eye Lia catches a glimpse of one, so full it's almost dragging its belly along the tarmac. It's an accordion bus – it has that creaky, bendy rubber bit in the middle – and there are people clinging to the steps and to its three wide-open doors, a bit like bees swarming to a hive.

Everyone on the passing buses can see her and Comrade Blaga walking home hand in hand.

The river is far below. Murky as always, barely moving along.

Mother explained that it used to be higher up and wild, liked to burst its banks whenever there was heavy rain, flooding houses, shops and roads, and so the people made it live in this river-gutter instead. If the shopkeeper were not still holding her hand, Lia would be leaning over the railing, throwing pebbles into the trapped river.

It's Mother's birthday today and she has no present.

Lia couldn't believe her luck when she first spotted the vase with a big yellow sunflower painted on it, couldn't believe that it was something people could buy. And so today, Lia had pointed at it in the homeware shop, and Comrade Blaga took the banknote from her. He looked her up and down – it was then that the bad-belly feeling started – then he locked the door of his shop. There was no one else inside.

And now – no money, no vase, no hand.

'Who's this?' A man has stopped in front of them. He shields his eyes from the low March sun.

'Poor kid got lost in town. I'm delivering her to her parents,' Comrade Blaga says. For some reason, Lia is embarrassed to look up at his face as he speaks.

'Whose is she, then?' this other man asks.

She has briefly forgotten about her trapped hand, so is surprised when it hurts.

'Ah, some scatty neighbours of mine,' Comrade Blaga says. Another squeeze of her hand. 'What kind of parent lets their kid roam the streets? Lucky I know them.'

He never gave back her money, and Mother's present is still on the shelf in the shop, high up so no children can break the precious yellow sunflower. She could tell this to the other man, who is staring at her. The problem is that although she does not remember being lost, she is not sure about that now, not sure at all. Maybe the bad feeling in her belly is the feeling of being lost.

'You're coming to the game, yes?' the other man says, by way of goodbye. He's already stepping past Lia and the shopkeeper.

'Don't I always?' Comrade Blaga replies.

Lia thinks of the cupboard at home that smells of foreign countries. This cupboard is in the living room, it's part of Grandpa's giant bookcase. It opens on creaky hinges like a trapdoor among the books, but usually it stays locked – it has a keyhole at the top, and there's an old, blackened key that Mother keeps in a porcelain cup in the glass bit at the top. The glass bit is not so tall that Lia can't reach the porcelain cup from a chair.

Just thinking about that cupboard usually cheers her up.

The shopkeeper stops, and Lia feels cool air on her hand. He moves to stand in front of her. He pats his coat and comes up with a handkerchief. He blows his nose, loudly. Wipes his nose with the handkerchief.

Lia pushes both her hands deep down into her pockets.

The shopkeeper grins at her. He pulls her right hand back out.

The cupboard, the cupboard. Mother and Dad keep the best, most colourful things in there: the chocolate from Germany – whenever a visitor has brought any – in shiny metal-foil wrapping, a glossy plastic shopping bag with pictures of fairy-tale creatures that Mother said are 'the zodiacs', a red fat bottle with a liquid that smells of bitter cherries and which

Mother and Dad sometimes take a sip from in matching tiny red glasses, a 'Kaleidoscope' tube, the most magical thing to ever exist and which Lia would never stop looking at except she's afraid she'll use up its colours and patterns, and underneath all this, the false cupboard bottom that she has spied Mother open through the bedroom-door keyhole. In it, some boring papers. And a very small pile of money.

But Lia meant to just think of the wonderful smell. All those different things have blended to create a special, sweet and oaky, cupboard perfume. She can smell it now in her mind, even though she is far from the cupboard. Nothing else smells like this.

No money, no present, no hand.

The small pile in the cupboard is supposed to be better than the regular money, and special money is what it takes to buy something as special as a yellow vase. The banknotes have complicated drawings, and beautiful, curly writing. Lia was tempted to colour in the hair and the face of the pretty woman that appears on some of the bills. But of course money is valuable and we cannot draw on it. Lia knows this, and she has never given in to the temptation of drawing on any money. Not even on the regular money.

'Who'll be at home, kid?' Comrade Blaga asks as they turn away from the river embankment and into her neighbourhood. 'Your mother? Your father? Both?'

If any of her friends are playing outside now, friends who went straight home after school instead of going to buy birthday presents, they will see her being walked home by this shopkeeper.

'Answer me. I know your mother, Silvia, you know? We went to gymnasium together.'

Lia is sure that the special banknote has already lost its magic-cupboard smell and now must just be smelling like the inside of the shopkeeper's pocket.

'Fine. It doesn't really matter. They're in too much trouble for it to matter.'

When she was very small, much smaller than now, she decided that she could see with her eyes closed, and the first thing that happened was that she walked nose-first into a lamp post.

'Stop that! Keep straight.' The man yanks at her hand.

As much as Lia tries to imagine herself inside the cupboard, her thoughts drag her back to that moment in the shop, the moment she handed the shopkeeper her banknote. Everything was perfect before then. She was sure the special banknote would be enough to pay for the vase, and she was sure Mother would love her present. The shopkeeper and his hand didn't even exist before that moment.

Steps. They are walking up the steps to their block.

She knows every broken bit of cement here, every groove in the pavement. Sometimes, when she has chalk and draws on the pavement, she makes the holes part of her drawings: here's a gorge that a troll could be jumping over, or a watering hole for a drinking tiger.

'Stop. Dragging. Your feet.'

She has made a mistake. At some point, she made a mistake, and now there is this feeling in her belly and this man has her hand.

He opens the door of her block, they walk up the steps. One floor, two floors. Their doorbell. Waiting. The click of the lock. The door opens. It's Mother, looking happy-surprised. Lia remembers that there is no present.

'Good afternoon, Comrade. We need to have a word.'

Lia looks down at her feet. She feels Mother grab her hand and pull her to her side. Finally, her other hand is free.

'Did my daughter do something?' Mother asks.

'Someone certainly did something.'

Nobody speaks for a few moments then, and so Lia looks up. The shopkeeper is still standing in the doorway, but he is holding the pretty banknote in front of his belly. He nods. 'Your daughter just tried to buy stuff off me with foreign currency.' He is whispering.

Lia looks back down at her feet. Her hand, now in Mother's hand, is being squeezed again.

They go into the living room and forget about her. Lia crouches by the door in the hallway, below the coat hanger. She sits on her hands, tries to press her hands into the floor. Where did they put that whole unruly river, while they were digging his gutter? The digging works must have taken many days.

When Mother and the shopkeeper come back out Mother no longer looks surprised-happy. The shopkeeper sees Lia on the floor and smiles. 'I just noticed – your mother has such green fingers! All the plants in here, a picture of good health. She will come over to my place now and again, help me with mine.'

Lia turns away from them both. She buries her face in Mother's long coat. The fabric is still cold from the outside;

Mother must have got in just before they arrived. If this were a day in which she had not been to the shops, Lia would now be washing her hands and getting ready for a snack – sometimes bread with honey cut up in little soldiers, sometimes bread and milk.

She hears the man sigh. 'Spare me that face, Comrade,' he says. 'Count yourself lucky I've no interest in little girls.'

The door closes. Lia, her face still buried in the cold coat, hears Mother's breathing next to her. If only she had brought the vase. Every time Lia had imagined the yellow vase on their table it was like looking at a small sun in the middle of their living room, at happiness itself.

2

Pitești, March

His wife didn't have to schedule classes so early on a Sunday morning, but schedule them she did. The phone shouldn't be ringing so early on a Sunday morning, but by God it does. Constantin stumbles out of bed and reaches the hallway.

'I've called three times now . . .' It's Davidescu, his boss. 'What the hell is that racket?'

'Sorry, I think I told you – my wife's a music teacher.'

'What a pain,' the police chief says. Then, 'The dirt road to the Old Gorge, just before the well. Get there now.'

'What's going on?' Constantin asks.

'A dirt road at the crack of dawn,' the police chief says. 'What do you think is going on, Beethoven's Fifth?' He hangs up.

Repetitive and wrong, the piano notes keep ringing out from the living room. It's a miracle the neighbours aren't banging the pipes in protest. Constantin cracks the door open: Tina and a girl in school uniform are at the piano, their backs to him. Tina is dressed in black, she always is.

'From the beginning,' Tina tells the girl.

He shuts the door back on the joyless notes.

His son comes running, also still in his pyjamas, and glues himself to his father's leg. Constantin hoists Sandu up on his right shoulder and pretends he's dealing with a bag of cement. The boy squeals with delight.

He changes quickly and brings his coffee with him to the car. It's chicory really, ersatz coffee. The thing is bitter and black but otherwise entirely unlike coffee; so far it has resisted attempts at being loved. Sometimes Tina, who doesn't even like real coffee, will drop a brick of it on the kitchen table without saying a word. It's understood then that a pupil paid her in coffee, that it's not a bribe in the strict sense of the word, and that he's free to drink it.

Today, though, it's a chicory day.

He stops the car about fifty metres from where a small crowd is gathered; slowly sips the tepid liquid. He's looking at an ambulance, the old coroner, Titus, in his filthy lab coat, two paramedics leaning against the side of the vehicle sharing a cigarette, and three colleagues of his taking orders from Titus. Across the road, three gypsy kids, two boys and a girl, stand watching the goings-on. No sense of urgency, and no police chief. The body is in the ditch, hidden from view.

The day is clear and chilly; the mornings still hold frost.

He steps out of the car. They're about one kilometre outside of town, on a road that leads from a shanty suburb to a second-rate tourist attraction, a waterfall that's only really interesting during the snowmelt. Beech forest on one side, shrubland on the other. He looks down at the dirt: there might be tyre tracks if his colleagues haven't already walked all over them.

'What do we have?' he asks when he's close enough to see into the ditch.

The body is on its back. It's a man in his fifties. He's wearing a pair of old boots, camouflage trousers and a sheepskin jacket. A bucket hat is on the ground next to him. There's blood.

'Hey!' The little gypsy girl suddenly runs up to them and turns a cartwheel on the ground behind the ambulance. She remains standing there with her arms and legs stretched out; star-shaped, grinning. She must be about seven, one day she will be eight. In an instant Constantin is all splintered heart.

He moves to block the child's view of the body.

'Scram!' Titus climbs out of the ditch and pretends to try to grab the girl; she flees, giggling.

The coroner then signals to the paramedics to move the body. 'Unless you want to have a look first?' he asks Constantin.

'ID?'

'Had it on him.' It's one of the police constables who answers. 'The injuries are just crazy. Can't even say who or what killed him,' the constable adds. 'Could be anything – man, machine or beast.'

Titus the coroner wipes his hands on the front of his already bloodstained coat and smiles wryly.

They hear gunshots then, from far inside the forest. Constantin looks at the coroner. 'Hunters,' Titus shrugs.

'It's not hunting season,' Constantin says.

11

Titus raises an eyebrow. 'They didn't tell you? Comrade Ceaușescu is here for the weekend. A little bear-hunting party.'

Constantin immediately jumps down into the ditch; he motions to the ambulance driver to get away from the body.

A loud whistle stops everyone in their tracks. 'This corpse may be a damned mess,' Titus says once he has their attention, 'but the one thing I'm sure of is he wasn't shot, not by . . .' the coroner points sideways, presumably in the direction of the hunting estate. 'Don't look at me like that. Do you know what bear shot is like? It runs a tunnel through you.'

The coroner makes a gesture as though he's punching a hole through the air.

Three hours later Constantin's at the station; he has asked Vasile, the police constable, to work on a Sunday until they can confirm the ID of the victim. Mainly, he wants to know if the man lived nearby, otherwise they'll need to work out what he was doing out there at night.

It's just the two of them in the office and it's cold. At some point Davidescu, the police chief, stops by; he says little, asks questions, leaves an open packet of Kent on Constantin's desk, and just hangs around the office smoking and looking over their shoulders as they work. The room slowly fills with smoke.

Constantin is looking at the Polaroids that Titus has sent over. In the photos, the body is naked and washed. The coroner was right: these are not bullet wounds, and there are no exit holes. Just those deep gashes on the torso. They don't look like knife wounds either; the edges are not sharp enough. Titus said he needs to think about it, he offered no immediate guess. Even

the angles are unhelpful: *not consistent with a stabbing motion.*
But the coroner is sure the crime happened in that spot, at
some point between midnight and the very early hours of the
morning. The ground underneath the body was blood-soaked.

'He was some kind of instructor at the trade school,' Vasile
says as he hangs up the phone. 'Carpentry, or something like
that. Married. Lives down by the stadium.'

Davidescu, who has been listening to them, puffs on his
cigarette, loudly. 'Remind me, why do people murder people?'
he asks.

'Money or sex or . . . politics?' Vasile hesitates, unsure presumably that he's allowed to say that last word.

'Alcohol. Mental illness. Injustice, actual or perceived,'
Constantin mutters, and goes on filling in the case file, adding
the latest bits of information.

'Why are you so damn proper?' Davidescu suddenly asks
him, still pacing the office. 'Women fancy you,' Davidescu
goes on, 'though I don't see why. Too soft, if you ask me.
Undecided. You look like someone who had second thoughts
in the middle of a fuck. But hey, they like you and that's that.
So, why so proper? And why that cold fish of a wife?'

Constantin winces at the insult. He's thinking how to answer
when he notices a glaring mistake in the file: the place where
they found the body is recorded as a roadside picnic area several
kilometres from where they were today.

'You got the location wrong,' he tells Vasile, and is about to
cross it out, when Davidescu says, 'Leave it. Makes our lives
easier.'

'Saying it happened in the wrong place?'

'It's a body in a ditch by the side of the road. Does it matter? This ditch or that ditch?'

'But – the witnesses. We'll be asking people about the wrong place.'

'You can ask about any place you want,' Davidescu says, 'just move the official murder site. I guarantee you'll have more trouble interrogating anyone if you keep saying it happened within pissing distance of the President's hunting party.'

It is evening already by the time Constantin and Vasile arrive at the victim's home to speak to his wife. Constantin is tired, his concentration is gone, and this meeting could have waited until the next day. But it's the kind of task that he would push into the geological future unless he gets it over with right away.

'It's so cold,' the woman says, wringing her hands. Then, 'Please take some.'

They are in her living room, sitting either side of a small serving trolley. The woman has placed a bowl of Turkish delight between him and Vasile and now and again she nudges it towards them. She sits across from them on the sofa, dressed in two housecoats, one over the other, and thick trousers tucked into wool socks. She is around fifty. Her face is puffy from crying.

The TV is on, the volume too high. Children are singing. The Ceauşescu-praising anthems fill the room.

'Mişu was going fishing, he went every Sunday. It was his small pleasure.'

Vasile has asked what her husband was doing on the out-skirts of town at that early hour.

14

'We didn't find any fishing tackle near the scene,' Vasile says.

'He was always going with friends,' she says. 'Maybe he was borrowing equipment from them?'

She shakes her head and starts crying; quietly, apologetically.

'We'll need the names and employment of your husband's fishing friends,' Vasile says.

The woman leaves the room, and Constantin takes the opportunity to look around. He has to go into many homes, sometimes to search them, and he is always taken aback by how similar they are. People's small hiding places, where they have a rest, what they want visitors to admire. A contraband case once took him all the way to a home in the north, by the Russian border, where he found the same stripy blanket, the same chess set doubling as a valuables box, the same kitchen cupboards and the same Chinese porcelain fisherman as in every home here.

The woman returns with an address book that she hands to Vasile.

It's true, Constantin thinks: there's just one kind of every object being produced, and nothing is imported. He wonders if this sameness is really just about limited resources and national saving targets, or if something more sinister is afoot. If there's an ultimate goal of making all their homes interchangeable. Maybe one day they will all have one identical key, and bunk down for the night in whatever apartment is nearest.

Constantin's fingers are itching to write down this thought. But he can't escape, not in the middle of this.

'Did your husband have any enemies?' Constantin asks the woman. He pauses for a moment to wait out the high notes of a Dear Leader song on the TV. 'Did he mention any serious arguments?'

She pulls a handkerchief from her sleeve and blows her nose. Shakes her head. 'You know what people are like,' she says, 'but my Mişu would never take anything that wasn't his.'

'There was a conflict, then?'

'Dear God, we've been having this awful trouble about the garage . . .'

She is telling them about a dispute with one of their neighbours when the ceiling light suddenly goes out. The TV, too; it flares white in an apparent fit of adulation, only to then crackle and die away to black.

A power cut. They are left sitting in darkness.

The woman apologises, tells them to stay put. They hear her stand up and leave the room. Soon a cold, weak light approaches from the hallway, and she returns with an oil lamp that she places on the serving trolley.

Constantin wishes he were somewhere far, far away.

Vasile takes down the details of the garage dispute. As they finish, it occurs to Constantin that the woman now looks expectant, somehow; it's as though she is waiting for instructions.

'We were told that there would be some kind of pension,' she says finally, her glance shifting from Constantin to Vasile. 'For, you know, Mişu's unofficial work. I mean, I have his Labour Card for his teaching, but I don't think he ever received any documents for the other job.'

'What other job?' Vasile asks.

'The . . . reports. You know,' the woman says.

Haltingly, the woman starts explaining about 'unconstitutional activities' and 'hostile elements among staff and students'. 'Constant watchfulness,' she says. 'It's what they told him.'

'Ah, I get it, one of us,' Vasile eventually says.

Is he imagining it, or did Vasile actually wink at him?

'That's not one of us,' Constantin says, as calmly as he can muster. 'What the Comrade describes is a Securitate informer.'

Constantin takes out the green ink pen and notebook from his breast pocket. By this light, no one can see what he's writing. *One kingdom, one key*, he starts. Somewhere in the distance he hears Vasile explain to the woman that they are the police, they are not investigating political crimes, and remuneration for any service her husband performed for '. . . er . . . the country . . .' will have to be dealt with by the same authority that commissioned his reports.

The following Tuesday Constantin goes looking for Titus down in the bowels of the university, and finds the coroner in the middle of demonstrating something to a huddle of pale kids. Constantin wonders if it's only first-year students who have to take Titus's classes – whenever he visits they're always so young. Or maybe, he thinks, no one at the university ever moves beyond this 'Titus and corpses' freshman experience. It wouldn't surprise him.

He takes a seat in the cold auditorium and tries to ignore the smell. A boy with fluff for a moustache is standing to the side of the table where the corpse is laid out. He's holding a pair of enormous shears. They're dripping blood on to his shoes.

The poor kid looks entirely absent, as if he has successfully vacated his body for the purpose of this class.

Constantin buries his freezing hands in his armpits. He would be writing, were it not so cold. He closes his eyes and tries to think of distant lands.

'. . . and here, just behind the left eyeball, we find the tumour,' Titus is saying, 'an orbital tumour to be precise. See how the growth has displaced the optic nerve?'

The show ends with Titus lifting the cadaver's head by the hair. Since Constantin sat down, several kids have fainted or thrown up. The smell of sick mingles with that of iron and putrefaction.

'Introductory Torment,' Constantin says to Titus when it's just them and a staff cleaner in the auditorium. 'Basic Gore,' he adds. Titus looks very much like a slightly older Kojak, and wears his blood-stained lab coat with the same panache as the TV cop wears his suits. The kids must be terrified of him.

'Small pleasures and all that.' Titus shrugs, removes his gloves.

'We've got to make sure to leave final instructions for our bodies not to end up in your hands.'

Constantin has only made a feeble joke, so he's taken aback when Titus unsmilingly answers, 'I'd say you've got more than enough on your plate worrying about the living.'

Is that an innuendo? Does he want to ask? In the event it doesn't matter: Titus's direct gaze has the effect of weakening Constantin's resistance against the sights and smells of the auditorium, against everything, and suddenly he, too, is shivering and bending over a bucket.

Titus hands him a towel, and waits by his side until the convulsions subside.

They move on to business. Constantin lays out the Polaroids of Sunday's victim. He asks if Titus has had any more thoughts about the injuries.

'Must have been something like a hook, in between a hook and a claw. See that edge? Sharper than a hook but not as sharp as a blade. About fifteen centimetres in length.'

'A DIY weapon?'

Titus shrugs. 'Maybe. I'm thinking something like a grappling hook. Mountaineering equipment, you know? And your man is strong. We've got seven wounds in all that are more or less equal in depth. That arm did not grow tired.'

Grappling hook! In dreams in which he's chasing suspects, when the time comes to shoot, Constantin finds he's unable to do it. The trigger becomes impossibly heavy. He counts himself lucky never to have tested his service weapon in real life. How can anyone go through the motion of hacking at another human?

Grappling hook. Heavy as a million triggers.

He still feels shivery after throwing up. He steadies himself before going on. 'Let's look at it the other way. What can you say with complete confidence?'

But Titus is still thinking about the weapon. 'A hook would also go some way to explaining the angles. Anyway.' The coroner then repeats most of the things that he has already told Constantin: no signs of struggle, the crime scene is the place where the body was found, no common toxins in the body.

'Does it remind you of anything?' Constantin asks. 'Ever

come across anything similar? I've asked for a list of all recently released violent criminals.'

Constantin says out loud whatever he knows so that Titus knows it, too. Speaking with Titus is another way of making facts stick, preventing them from being lost. Two minds remember better than one.

Titus is sceptical. 'Anyone caught doing this kind of thing would've hanged.'

Constantin considers this. 'Maybe against animals? Or just a very violent assault – a failed murder.'

'None of that would've crossed my desk.'

'The guy was an informer,' Constantin says.

Titus shrugs. 'You know where to look, then.'

Constantin has already requested and read the dead man's Securitate file, and he has also asked the Securitate if this informer's reports resulted in any kind of punishment for the people he snitched on. Did his reports cause sufficient damage for someone to want to hack him to death? A Securitate archivist sent him a dry fax in reply, saying that his victim had reported on a student selling Deutsche Marks on the black market who got expelled. Five years ago. Nothing else.

'But the guy now works in the Ploieşti refinery and seems to have been out of town for weeks,' Constantin explains to Titus. 'His parents told me he'll be back this Friday. I'll see him.'

'You talked to anyone else?' Titus asks.

'The widow and a neighbour he was arguing with.' Constantin tells Titus that the garage dispute is with an ancient, retired professor. Can hardly lift his walking stick. 'The three fishing buddies,' he adds, 'who always travel to the river together and have mutual alibis.' Constantin shakes his head. 'No luck so far.'

He doesn't say that Davidescu also wants him to speak to the prostitutes known to hang out by the roadside picnic area, the wrong but by now official murder site. It's stupid, a complete waste of time, but his boss is insisting out of some perverse impulse. *Saint versus Sinner, I want to see that movie*, Davidescu had said, pretending to frame a billboard with his hands. *These career girls will know all that moves around that car park. It's a clear dereliction of duty for you to neglect a potential witness.*

'I'll have another go at the body,' Titus says. 'But I think it's legwork that will solve this one.'

By way of goodbye Constantin says, 'I was joking earlier, you know. About the gore. I know the kids need to toughen up.'

Titus won't have it. 'If you want to talk about something, just come out with it. Dissection is the name of the class.'

At home that evening Constantin slumps in an armchair in front of the TV. He feels a bit nauseous. In fact, he thinks he can somehow still catch a whiff of the awful dissection-room smell. He brings his palms to his nose, sniffs at them with his eyes closed.

He contemplates making the effort of getting up to wash his hands again.

Tina is at the sewing machine, mending a pair of overalls for Sandu. The plasticky sewing machine and the stately piano look out of place next to one another in their tiny living room; Constantin can imagine struggling piano pupils being asked to move to the less demanding instrument.

Tina is constantly busy, has to be. Left to herself she would schedule teaching at all hours of day and night, and when he mentions neighbours and quiet hours, she says they haven't complained. But obviously they wouldn't. He's a cop.

'Fairy-tale night tonight!' Sandu jumps up on the armchair and makes a nest for himself by his father's side.

Tina taps her wristwatch.

'It only takes a few minutes,' Constantin says. 'Then we'll go to bed, yes?' he waits for Sandu's approval.

Tina straightens her back at the sewing machine, takes a deep breath, then gets up and leaves the room. Sandu follows her with his eyes. The boy still worries about them, but he has stopped asking if they are 'upside down'.

He and Tina create many small problems, he knows, behind which they hide the monster problem.

'Are we ready, then?' Constantin asks Sandu, before standing up and bringing the notebook with the fairy tales to the armchair.

'What's it going to be about?' Sandu asks.

It's so easy and wonderful, this age. Sandu's age. Constantin has to teach him things like wash your hands, don't stick your hand into the dog's mouth, eat your food. No difficult lessons yet.

'This, believe it or not, is a story about hats.'

He writes these whimsical stories at the office, in between tasks or during Davidescu's monologues, in a funny green ink with pens that he once confiscated from a black market dealer. Happy, impossible stories. They'll leave him alone at the office if he's seen writing, and so he writes. Green, now, to him, is the colour of freedom. He still has enough of the green ink pens for about two more notebooks.

'I hope there's a prince,' Sandu says.

Constantin squeezes him tight.

'Once upon a time there was a little hamlet where there lived a small, happy jeweller. One day our little jeweller went out for a stroll and saw that quite a few people in his village had taken to wearing a sort of funny, pointed hat; a bit like the kind that wizards wear, but with a smaller brim. The jeweller thought they looked extremely silly. But soon after that, his wife came home from the market wearing one of these hats, almost covering up her beautiful eyes. She chirped that she had bought one for him, too.

'He didn't like his present. He told his wife she could wear the hat as much as she wanted, but he didn't like having anything on top of his head. Besides, the hat was useless on windy days, or when it rained. The water would just run down the cone and on to your face.

'The fashion spread and spread, and soon there wasn't a person within a day's riding who didn't wear the hat. The children, too: the town decided that the children would get their first hat at the traditional coming-of-age ceremony, and the day would be known as the Holy Hat Gift day.

'The sight of all the silly cones everywhere was infuriating. And because the hat trade was going so well, many of the town's shops turned into hat shops. The little jeweller wondered where all the housewives now went for their bread.

'Those who walked into the little jeweller's shop seemed to flinch when they saw his bare head. They reacted as though he were naked. People also seemed to need fewer rings and bracelets, and when the jeweller looked at his accounts, his fears were confirmed. Business was suddenly terrible.'

Constantin's thoughts drift to the widowed woman trying to collect the pension due to her informer husband. He wonders vaguely how that will go, whether the Securitate keeps its promises. If even an institution as powerful as that is afraid the rumour will spread that they don't reward loyalty.

'Daddy?' Sandu says.

'Sorry. Where were we? Yes – every few days the jeweller's wife tried to convince him that the hat was for his own good. She told him about the town's butcher, who was the only other resident still rejecting the hat. Someone had painted threats and insults on the butcher's front door, and broken a window, and the butcher had left town. "Lord knows where he went, they have the hat everywhere," his wife said.

'The town's priest came to see the little jeweller. The people in the town were concerned, the priest said. What did he have against them? *Why is our hat not good enough for you, when it is good enough for us?*

'Soon afterwards, the jeweller's wife came home crying. Because of her husband's bare head she was being shunned by the other women in town. She had no friends left, she said. They'd be chased out of town soon, she fretted, just like the butcher.'

'The following day, the little jeweller got up early and locked himself in his workshop, and spent the whole day in there, cutting, gluing and hammering away; worrying his wife. When he came out, she couldn't believe her eyes: he was wearing a hat, the most beautiful hat she had ever seen. Her husband knew how to shape all sorts of materials and had made a truly astonishing object, adorned with emeralds and rubies on yellow silk. The new hat was a little smaller than the traditional hats – only a little, a few centimetres in height and width, so that the smaller size, together with the much more delicate craftwork, seemed to ennoble rather than diminish the revered object.

'The little jeweller went out for a walk and got an enthusiastic reception. The next day his shop was full. Everyone wanted to order a hat like his. His reputation as a master hat-maker spread rapidly around the country, and everyone who was anyone came to the town to have their hats made by the little jeweller.'

Constantin suddenly has a thought: for all the talk and fear of Securitate, he has never actually met anyone identified as such, nor had any kind of direct contact with them. There's the odd time that Davidescu does communicate an order allegedly received from them, but Constantin suspects that mostly it's about what someone high up thinks the Securitate want the police to do, rather than any direct involvement. He thinks, really, we're secret-policing ourselves. Where are they?

'Again? Daddy.' Sandu taps his arm.

'This was just to see if you're paying attention,' he winks at Sandu. 'So. The only problem now was that some people complained that they could not afford the new hat. With all the decorative stones and silk, it was too expensive. The little jeweller sympathised with them; after all, everyone should be able to afford a holy hat. So he made the next model even smaller, and after a while, the very smallness of the hat became the hallmark of superiority. Hat manufacturers everywhere endeavoured to keep up with fashion and tried to copy the little jeweller's design. They couldn't make their hats more beautiful than the jeweller's, but they could certainly make them smaller. After a few years the holy hats had become so small that from a distance you could hardly spot the cone on a man's head. At that size, the little hats were inconvenient. They got lost, too, and with all the money people had spent on the stones that adorned the hats, they felt they were safer in the display case at home than atop anyone's head.

'When the jeweller was so old that he had to start thinking of closing his little shop, he went to the coming-of-age ceremony of a friend's granddaughter. When the time came to place the hat on the girl's head, the priest merely patted the child's head and chanted a few words.

'Back home, the jeweller, a blissful smile on his face, gathered all his own and his wife's old hats and threw them in the rubbish bin outside, and the people who passed him on the street didn't even blink. And still today he's in a rocking chair outside his shop, merrily waving to all the hatless people.'

Sandu is quiet; probably still waiting for a prince to appear. Constantin closes the notebook.

'The poor jeweller. All that compulsive hat-making and you didn't like his story.'

'Were they warm hats?' Sandu asks. 'Mama always wants me to wear a hat when it's cold outside.'

'I guess they were stupid hats.'

'It wasn't a very good story, Dad.' Sandu looks up at him, puts out a hand and strokes his cheek; once, twice.

He kisses the top of the boy's head. 'Our audience is our master. No more hats.'

A couple of hours later, Constantin is in bed but still not properly asleep. His breathing is fretful. He has been going over the case in his mind, drifting in and out of sleep. He's still uncomfortably aware of the widow's pain, but then he remembers what he knows about the man – the husband she mourns was reporting on colleagues' and students' harmless jokes, or their complaints about the food shortages. The man she was crying over would go home after work, write a report, and the following week a colleague of his would receive a visit from the Securitate.

But he really is tired, and slowly he loses track of what's real and what's dream. The corpse that Titus had been dissecting at the university wasn't the man in the ditch, it's got nothing to do with the case, and yet now, in this half-conscious state, the corpse, the murdered informer, the widow, they are all one bloody mess, and the stench that Constantin can't shake is their foul secret.

3

Sighișoara, March

Lia is on the bus home from school. Dad is with her. They are just passing along the riverbank, the murky river sulking down below the bus windows.

With her finger, Lia draws a circle in the grime on the glass, then another one. It's going to be a bicycle.

It's good she is with Dad because he's the one who doesn't really want to still be angry with her. Dad smiled at her earlier at the school gate, even mussed her hair before he remembered that he's supposed to be angry. She looks up at him now. He has some bits of dirt – grass? – in the hair at the back of his head.

He sees her looking and wipes it off. 'Been out all day measuring inclinations on a damn field. I don't know which way is up right now.'

He might let her do the competition.

Since the day of the shopkeeper Mother and Dad have not let Lia walk home by herself. It's been two weeks, and they haven't let her do much at all. School, homework, eat, sleep. She always gets some punishment when she's been bad, but not like this. This time the punishment is everywhere.

The 'problem family' on the third floor comes to her mind, with the father who beats the children so hard Lia can hear their cries two floors down. Maybe it's not so bad. They would hear her cry up there, for a little while, and that's it. Punishment over.

'Dad, there's this drawing competition,' she says. 'I just need some coloured chalk. It's not expensive.'

'A competition?' Dad says.

'I can win a red bike.' She repeats Comrade Cauliflower's words from earlier in the day: *Our town will host a regional chalk-drawing competition. The theme, 'The Communist Paradise', allows for many creative interpretations. You children have three weeks to prepare yourselves. The first prize is the world-famous Pegasus bicycle.*

Dad looks like he's thinking about it.

'Who's it for?' he says. 'This competition. Who's in it?'

'Comrade Sava said it's the whole school, Dad. All the kids.' Lia is not allowed to say 'Comrade Cauliflower' out loud, even though Dad said that, yes, the teacher's hair does look like a cauliflower.

Dad shrugs. 'I'll speak to your mother.'

'I can do it? Really?'

'If it's the whole school, I don't see how we can keep you out of it and not have trouble.'

Lia leans up and kisses him on the cheek. He smiles.

The thing is, Dad also thinks Mother is too angry for what happened. He told Lia as much the other evening, when she was crying because Mother still wouldn't come to kiss her goodnight. *I don't know. In the end, kid, you made a stupid mistake. But nothing happened. That Blaga fellow didn't call the police. Your mother is just frightened of what could have been. It'll pass.*

The worst part was that they didn't say what she did wrong. Not really. They said it was because she took the money, and without asking, but they know she didn't take it for herself. How could she ask them if the money was for Mother's surprise birthday present? It should all be easy to understand. Instead, when Lia told Mother to go to the shop and see for herself that the vase was bright yellow, that it would have been the most beautiful thing in their house, Mother slapped her.

Sometimes it's like they are trying to keep a secret from her, but at the same time they're angry that she doesn't guess what it is.

She has another go at the drawing on the bus window. The problem is the bike in her head is shiny and red, and there's no way of getting that across with a finger-drawing on grime.

'The Communist Paradise,' Lia whispers to herself.

She draws two bendy lines – the Pegasus's high, arched handlebars – then the two thick tyres.

For the competition, she thinks, she's going to draw something like a circus, or a jungle full of the best animals. The ones with even their bottoms brightly coloured.

At home, Dad barely has time to put the key inside the lock when the door flies open and Mother appears, looking very upset. Her eyes are red.

'Silvia . . .' Dad says, but Mother pulls them both inside in a hurry and closes the door. She hugs Dad like he's been away forever.

Lia, who was just about to blurt out everything about the competition, stops herself. She tries to join in, put her arms around Mother and Dad's hug.

'You shouldn't have done it!'

Mother's voice is strange. Lia looks up at her – Mother really is crying.

'What's going to happen to us?' Mother goes on.

Dad grabs Mother by the shoulders. 'What's this about? Silvia. What's going on?'

Mother, still sobbing, looks at Dad in a strange way, like she's trying to see behind his eyes.

'Silvia!' Dad shakes her. 'What's going on?'

Mother blows her nose. 'You don't have to pretend with me,' she says quietly.

'For God's sake! What are you talking about?'

'He's dead,' Mother whispers. 'That Blaga devil. Murdered. The whole neighbourhood is talking about it.'

When Lia thinks about the shopkeeper she gets the bad-belly feeling. So she never thinks about him. There are two fairy-tale books that Lia is afraid of, ones with terrible end-ings, and these books sit at the bottom of the pile of books at the back of her and Dani's book cupboard, and she never takes them out. This is how she feels about the shop and the shopkeeper. She will never go near the place, never look at him, never think of him again. He's at the bottom of the pile of people.

Dad lets his arms fall. Mother hugs him again. 'I would

have dealt with it, I swear. I would have found a way out. You shouldn't have done this.'

Dad steps back from Mother. He walks past both of them, goes into the living room. Sits down in the armchair.

He hasn't taken off his coat.

Mother is trying to stop crying. Lia grabs hold of Mother's hand. Mother doesn't even notice.

'Blaga was killed?' Dad says.

Lia is thinking about how Dad shouldn't be sitting in the living room in his coat. Then Mother's hand slips out of hers, and Mother goes to sit on the sofa next to Dad.

'But you know that, Victor,' Mother says.

Dad is staring at Mother. He opens his mouth to speak. Nothing comes out. Then he rubs his eyes with the fingers of one hand. He only does that when he is very angry, and trying very hard not to hit Lia.

'And you think I had something to do with it?' Dad finally says.

It's a competition about paradise, Lia wants to say. *Stop this talk. A drawing competition! I can use all the colours.*

'Silvia,' Dad says. 'Answer me. Why on earth would you think that?'

Why isn't Mother answering? Why does she look afraid?

'Victor . . .'

'You told me the fellow brought our daughter home after she tried to buy stuff in his shop with Deutsche Marks.' Dad speaks in a slow, angry whisper.

Mother has covered her face with her hands. She is shaking her head.

Another question pops up in Lia's head: how do mothers and fathers kiss and hug their children again after they beat them? It must be strange.

'Answer me. The man could have gone straight to his pals at the Securitate, but he gave us a break. Why the hell would anyone want to kill a man for that?'

Mother is rocking slowly on the sofa. Shaking her head.

Lia has backed away from them and is pressing against the cold radiator.

Dani comes into the room then, Lia's little brother. He's clutching a crust of bread. There's purple jam on his hand and around his mouth. He walks over to Dad and reaches up across the armrest to stuff the crust into Dad's mouth.

Dad hasn't noticed Dani is there and the bread drops from his mouth. Only when the bread crust is in his lap does Dad turn to Dani, looks at him as if it's the first time he's seen him. He pushes him aside.

Dad doesn't look angry any more, but somehow it's worse.

'Are you saying . . . ?' Dad says.

The jam-smeared bread crust is still in Dad's lap. Mother is still covering her face with her hands. Dad's face . . . Lia has to look away. It's as if night has fallen in the living room.

That whole day, nobody speaks to anybody again and nobody looks at anybody. And the next morning it's the same. At breakfast, Dani starts crying for no reason, like he was doing when he was a baby. He eats like that, sobbing, with snot running into the plate, and Mother keeps telling him in a mean voice to stop or he'll choke on his soldiers. It's like it's not Mother. Like she can't see that the way she says it just makes Dani's crying worse.

Dad comes into the kitchen and drinks a glass of water.

'The main thing is it wasn't you,' Mother says. She's talking to Dad without turning to look at him. 'I was about to lose my mind,' she says.

Dad slams the glass on the kitchen counter so hard a cupboard flies open. 'When the hell were you going to tell me?' He still has his back to them.

Mother closes her eyes.

'And whose idea was it to keep the money there, with stuff she's obsessed by?' Dad goes on. 'With a goddamn toy. With chocolates.'

'It was locked!' Mother almost screams. 'And hidden.'

'Of all the fucking places.'

Dad turns and looks at Lia's empty plate. 'You're done. Get out of here,' he says.

It's Sunday, and after breakfast normally Lia would ask if she can go out and play, but she's afraid to speak. She gets up from the table. She doesn't know what to do with herself. She goes around the apartment once and ends up sitting on the floor in the hallway.

'Please. Please let's forget it,' Lia hears Mother's voice in the kitchen.

Someone moves in there then and suddenly Lia can only hear a man's loud, shouty football commentary. They've turned on the radio.

Lia remembers her hand that day, trapped in the shopkeeper's fist. She knows she should think about what happened, try to understand, but the whole thing is like a scary monster inside her, and her thoughts are little cowards who run and hide under the table. She had an idea of setting it up like one of those mathematics sentences at school, where the answer plops out at the other end. On one side she has Mother and Dad's anger, plus her own bad-belly feeling, plus the special money, plus the yellow vase. But her thoughts still don't want to go anywhere near it.

The doorbell rings then. Mother comes out of the kitchen, steps over Lia's legs to get to the front door.

Two men come in. Lia is so surprised by their uniforms, by how strange it is to see the uniformed men in their house, that she misses what they say, and only hears the answer – 'But why?' – and then, though it was Mother speaking, with Mother's voice, Lia decides it must have been someone else, maybe someone she can't see outside their front door who sounds like a frightened, helpless child.

Dad comes out of the kitchen too, takes a big step over her legs.

It's almost like you're somewhere else entirely, Lia thinks, when you sit on the floor far below other people's talk. If she doesn't look up and they don't look down, they would not be bothering each other at all. She notices that the edge of the carpet has come unstuck in a spot by the wall, and she pokes at it with her finger, tests if it will come away enough for her to see what's underneath. Then she lies down to look under the shoe cupboard, and spots a ping-pong ball she had thought was lost.

The next time she looks up, the policemen are still there,

and Mother and Dad are coming out of the bedroom dressed in town clothes. They open the door and let the policemen out. Then, still without really looking at her and Dani, Dad says that they'll be back in a few hours. Instead of giving her the key, they shut the door.

The key turns in the lock from the outside. Lia cannot believe it, but that's what happens.

What about fire, she wants to shout, what if there's a fire? Mother always says we are never supposed to lock anyone in. There could be a fire. Mother said so herself.

They'll remember and come back. For a while she waits by the door with Dani crouched at her feet.

Nothing.

'We must check on the stove,' she tells Dani.

Stove and oven are off. Lia stretches on her toes and makes sure that the metal box where Mother throws the spent matches is empty.

Dani starts crying again.

'What are you crying for? We're going out, too,' Lia says.

She puts on her shoes and then helps Dani put his on. When they're done she takes his hand and they go inside the large wardrobe in their bedroom. She pulls the door shut by the little metal 'L' that's part of its lock. She closes her eyes. The wardrobe smells of all of Mother and Dad's perfumes, of naphthalene against the-cursed-moths, and of a resin that's nice and smooth to touch, not like the rest of the inside wood which is scratchy. The soft clouds under her and Dani are bags full of fabric odds and ends.

'Night again,' Dani whispers.

They're sitting as if in a small rowing boat, facing each other. A boat at night, because it's so dark. 'I'm going to tell you a secret. We're in a fairy tale. But you can't tell anyone. Mother and Dad don't know,' Lia explains in a whisper. 'Bad people, they want to steal all the colours.'

It feels good saying it. Dani starts sobbing again. She strokes his foot. 'Don't be afraid.' It's a fairy tale, she thinks, so of course the good people will win in the end. Then she remembers the two terrible books, the ones she will never take out from the bottom of the pile of books.

She will not think about them.

'We're waiting for a message,' she tells Dani. In fairy tales, the hero usually receives a message so he knows what needs to be done.

'I want Mama,' Dani sobs.

Lia doesn't know what to say. If it's the really scary kind of fairy tale, it's possible Mother and Dad will never come back. She hopes Dani hasn't had this thought.

'There's still some colour,' she says. Easter is in two weeks, with the coloured eggs that she always tries to keep until they smell so bad that Mother makes her throw them straight into the big bin outdoors. Once spring is back there's going to be green grass and flowers. The chalk-drawing competition.

'The really bad things,' she says, 'they only happen when all the colour's gone.'

The next day she walks home from school by herself, and falls into an argument with her feet about going straight home or passing by the shop where they sell the coloured chalk. I have no money, she keeps telling her feet, and they say you're just going to have a look. Mother and Dad will be furious, she tells them, and they say Mother and Dad are not even looking at you.

Her nose touches the stationery shop window, and she cups her hands, trying to see the shelves behind the counter where they keep pencils, watercolours and chalk. There's no point going in. Mother came back home yesterday after a few hours, without the policemen and without Dad, but she did not talk to her. Lia found her dinner on the kitchen table and had to eat alone.

When she looks up she sees the old man from the tower block opposite theirs, what's his name? Comrade Mantea. He's also cupping his hands and peering inside the stationery shop.

'What?' Comrade Mantea says.

She was staring at him.

'Do you have any idea how dangerous this is?' He nudges her with his elbow. 'This is how queues start! You think you can just la-de-da innocently loiter in front of a shop?'

The old man winks at her. 'If we're not careful we'll soon have a braying mob on our hands. A stampede. All clamouring for' – he turns to look at the shop window again – 'grid-lined notebooks.'

This old man is making fun of her. Of the chalk she can't have, the competition she'll miss. The red bike that they'll give to some other child.

'Hey! What's this?' Comrade Mantea says. 'Don't cry, for God's sake. What's wrong?'

She tells him about the competition and the chalk that she

needs. That Dad promised her that she could take part, but then . . .

'Then what?' Comrade Mantea says.

She wipes her nose on the sleeve of her coat. 'They had to go into town,' Lia says.

Comrade Mantea looks at the shop, then at her. 'I'll get you the blasted chalk. Come on.'

The old man walks into the shop like it's his house.

They have just gone in when a woman, the first of two customers at the counter, asks for coloured chalk. Lia runs to the counter.

The saleswoman takes a bunch of cardboard boxes from a cabinet behind her. Lia recognises the boxes.

'The fourth person today to buy chalk. What on earth is going on?' the saleswoman asks while working the till.

'It's this chalk-drawing competition,' the customer replies. 'The kids are going crazy. They can win a bicycle.'

The next customer, a young man, only wants envelopes. Lia can breathe again.

'Two boxes of chalk for young Michelangelo here,' Comrade Mantea says when it's their turn.

The saleswoman bends down and from a cabinet next to the first one takes out two boxes. 'That will be seven lei,' she says, and puts them on the counter.

Comrade Mantea fiddles with his wallet. Lia pulls his sleeve, 'They're white! I need coloured chalk.' She points at the right cabinet.

'Sorry, we want the—'

'We're out of coloured chalk,' the woman says.

Comrade Mantea frowns. The saleswoman moves to stand in front of the little cabinet doors. Her hair looks like a helmet.

'I just saw you sell coloured ones,' Comrade Mantea says quietly.

'Next!' the saleswoman shouts.

Lia looks around. There is no one else in the shop.

'That was the last lot of chalk,' the saleswoman says.

'In that one, in there!' Lia shouts. She points at the right cabinet. 'Behind you!' she tells the saleswoman.

'Well?' Comrade Mantea says.

The woman doesn't move. 'If the foreman comes in wanting some chalk for his sons, I can't tell him there isn't any!' she says. 'Or the Comrade Director.'

'So. You still have chalk,' Comrade Mantea says.

'Chalk's out.'

'That's how it is now?' Comrade Mantea says. 'You lot are trying to profiteer even from kids' chalk?'

The saleswoman purses her lips and walks away from them.

'You have no shame!' Comrade Mantea shouts to the woman's back. He walks out of the store.

Lia runs after him. 'You saw! There were so many boxes left,' she tells Comrade Mantea.

She did not cry yesterday, or the day of the shopkeeper, but today she wants to cry all the time.

'Christ, I hate them,' Comrade Mantea says. He turns his face up at the sky and closes his eyes.

'She wants a gold brick,' Lia sobs.

'What are you talking about?'

Between sobs, she tells him about the bricks packed in

41

beautiful gold foil that Mother always has in her handbag when she's in town, just in case some shop is selling something worth buying. 'Or if we need the doctor, or papers from a, you know, an office.'

'You mean the coffee packets? Nobody in their right mind would trade coffee for chalk, kid.' Comrade Mantea goes quiet. He looks like he's thinking. 'Nope, nobody in their wrong mind either.'

She knows what he's going to say next. That it's not his fault, that her competition is not his problem.

'I'm on the second floor, apartment twelve,' Comrade Mantea says. 'Come tomorrow after five. I'll have your chalk. Can't let the bastards win!'

Dad arrives home at the same time as Lia, they meet on the staircase. He's unshaven and looks tired. His clothes are rumpled. When he has a little beard like that Lia usually strokes his cheek, but now she's afraid to take her hands out of her pockets.

Mother tells Lia her afternoon snack is in the kitchen and locks herself and Dad up in the living room. Lia plays with her food for a while, but then she takes her plate with the sandwich and goes to listen by the door.

'I'm so damn worried someone will remember they saw her walk home with him,' she hears Dad say. 'And they'll bring her in for questioning.'

'Victor, we stick to our story. If they ask a thousand times, that's what we say a thousand times.'

'You know, they said he was cut up like confetti,' Dad says. 'Whoever did it must have really hated the bastard.'

Silence.

'I guess that's the only lucky thing in this mess,' Dad again. 'The police have about twenty suspects. Everybody and his dog hated this fellow.'

They are quiet after this, or whispering. Lia is about to go back to the kitchen when she hears Dad say, 'The fucking shame!' followed by a crash, like something heavy breaking. Mother gives a shriek.

Lia bursts into the living room. She stops herself at the last moment from stepping on the shards of the glass ashtray that Dad brought from his trip to Kishinev.

'Comrade Sava asked me today if I've started practising for the competition,' Lia says. It's only half a lie – Cauliflower asked the whole class. 'Everyone has to take part. But I don't have any chalk.'

Mother and Dad stare at her.

'I just can't . . .' Mother says, and gets down on all fours to collect the shards. Eventually Dad puts his hand inside his suit jacket and takes out a ten-lei note. He gives it to Lia without a word.

'I can win a red bike,' Lia says.

Dad shakes his head. 'No,' he says. 'You can't win a red bike. Dora will win, or some other kid whose . . .' He stops. 'I don't want you to be disappointed.'

'But I'm better than her at this,' Lia says. Dora wins every prize, but this is drawing. Colours. Lia hates it that her voice is trembling.

Dad reaches out a hand and pulls her close to him. 'Listen to me for once. You will not win. It's not a real competition.'

43

'What's that food doing on the floor?' Mother says, and goes and picks up Lia's plate with the sandwich from the doorway. She yanks at Lia's hand and makes her hold the plate. Then she turns to Dad. 'That's right – why don't you ask your daughter what she was doing chatting to that Mantea lunatic.'

How is this possible, how does Mother know? She just left Comrade Mantea and the stationery shop.

Lia takes a bite out of the sandwich.

'Don't look so surprised,' Mother says. 'Comrade Popa saw you.'

'Lia,' Dad says. 'Why are you talking to that man?'

Lia remembers now, something about not being allowed to talk to this neighbour. She chews as slowly as possible.

'I was just looking at the chalks in the shop. He was there.'

Dad tilts his head the way he does when he doesn't believe you.

'I told him about the competition.'

'This child . . .' Mother says, and storms out of the room.

'Can't you just listen to us?' Dad says. 'If we ask you not to do something, it's important.'

Lia takes another big bite out of the sandwich. It's good sometimes, not being able to talk.

'Think about your brother,' Dad says. 'You don't want him to play with the hot iron, but you can't explain to him that he mustn't plug it in, or not push the "on" button, because then it becomes hot and will burn him. So you just tell him not to touch it, ever.'

'But I'm not little. You can tell me.'

Dad leans back in his armchair.

'I don't know how you have the patience!' Mother shouts from the bathroom.

'Listen. Old Mantea is not a bad person, he was a university professor, but he's crazy. He goes around saying crazy things. Things that, if I were to say them, I would end up in prison. But he has important relatives – the way your classmate Dora has important relatives, only Mantea's are even more important than our chief prosecutor. So nothing ever happens to him.'

Comrade Mantea did seem different, Lia thinks. The way he talked to the mean shop woman. The way he talks to her. Like he doesn't care, but in a good way. She likes it very much.

'Hey. You listening?' Dad pokes her. 'But they might arrest the people he is talking to, do you understand? That's why we don't want you to talk to him. It's not because of what you will say, it's because of what he might say. Tell me you understand this.'

That evening, in bed, Lia can't stop thinking about what Dad said. *It's not a real competition. You can't win.* She remembers the helmet woman at the stationer's: *Chalk's out!* The yellow vase, high up on its shelf, that can't be bought for any money.

It's just as bad as she thought. She checks on Dani next to her, but he's already asleep.

They really are in a fairy tale. Somebody's really stealing the colours. So many things make sense now. Everything that Grandpa left is more colourful than everything they have today. The old Christmas baubles, his books, the wooden toys. Why is that, when everybody still loves colour? People are happiest at Christmas and Easter and the National Day Parade. People buy beautiful flowers when they want to make someone happy, and the sun is the happiest-making thing of all. Nobody, nobody in the whole world, wants less colour.

She lies in the dark, her eyes wide open. She imagines a big, enormous vault, full to the brim with stolen colour, and an evil shadow squatting at the top.

It's Monday, Lia's at school, it's the long break, and the others are playing around her in the yard. She has just closed the lid of her lunchbox when she sees the two grey men in the window of the staffroom. Comrade Sava appears between the two. She points Lia out to them.

Lia has played hide-and-seek sometimes in the schoolyard, but it's not the best place for that. The yard is squarish with only some benches and a small playground in a corner. And every time, though she knows it's pointless, she wastes at least half the countdown on trying to come up with a better hiding spot, so that by the time the seeker shouts, 'Two, one, coming to get you!' the words ring out really loud and mean, and she has barely reached even a bench. A bench is the lousiest spot of all because they can see you through the slats.

'Hello, kid.'

The men are standing in front of her.

If only she had something to put in her mouth. She opens the lunchbox again. Sometimes she doesn't eat it all, or she leaves the apple for later, but today it was yellow cheese sandwich, which goes best with the apple. She's looking at crumbs.

'Put that away.'

One of the men takes the lunchbox, closes it, and puts it on the bench next to her. He sits down on the other side. 'We're going to ask you some questions, OK? You just need to tell us what you remember. You've got nothing to be afraid of. And if you're a good girl you'll get this.'

He waits for a while, then he nudges Lia with his elbow. She looks up at him. He's holding a stick of chewing gum.

She has done some bad things today already that they could ask about. In the first break of the day she told Dora what Dad had said – that they're going to give Dora the prize, just like that. She told Dora that it's unfair, like stealing, and made Dora cry, even though she likes Dora and doesn't really think she's the thieving kind. Another thing: she took the ten lei that Dad gave her and instead of trying the stupid stationery shop again, she went to Comrade Mantea's apartment, the old man that nobody talks to, and he really had her coloured chalk.

When she does something bad, Comrade Sava puts her in the corner, or she gets the ruler. Once she got the ruler twenty times.

'You remember the nice man who works in the homeware shop downtown? He walked you home one day.'

Slowly, so she doesn't upset the men, she takes the lunchbox back on to her lap. Everything is wrong. How is it possible never to think about something and it still doesn't go away?

'Listen, it's your parents who told us. They said to speak to you. We just want to hear what you remember.'

She remembers this: that it shouldn't have happened, that no one should have known, that she must not talk about it. If only Mother or Dad were here.

She thinks as hard as she has ever thought about anything, but every time her mouth is about to open, she clamps it shut.

Say the wrong thing, and Mother and Dad will never look at her again.

'How about just yes or no, all right? And you can tell us if you're not sure? Has that man ever been to your house?'

She tries, she really does. The bad thing about the bad day started from the money. She's sure she must not speak about the money. Maybe she could tell them about the rest of the day, but she's not sure. The money with the bad man, the bad man with Dad being furious, Dad being furious with these men: everything is stuck together. She can smell the sweetish cupboard smell now, that whole day smells like that in her head. It used to be a good smell.

'Or did your mum and dad lie to us?' the man asks. 'You didn't walk home with Comrade Blaga? You realise it's very serious if they lied to the police. Tell us it isn't so.'

The bell rings then. The bell means all the children have to return to class. Lia slides forwards a little on the bench. Nothing happens. She goes another little bit. Her toes are touching the ground now.

The man on the bench puts his arm in front of her, like a barrier. 'Your teacher knows you'll be late.'

'Actually, don't you think that damn teacher should've told us the kid's slow?' the other man says.

'Don't be like that. She's not slow.'

'Kid got her eyes closed like you're not sitting here, talking to her face.'

She remains seated like that, halfway down the bench, her toes touching the ground. It's going to be like this from now on. *Two, one, coming to get you,* but all the time.

'How about we just get the parents again? Let's get out of here. It's been thirty years and I still hate this place.'

She hears them walk away, but she doesn't move and doesn't open her eyes until she hears furious knocking on a window. It's Comrade Sava, who wants her back in class.

The day of the competition is a big, sunny day and Lia holds out her hand, turns her palm up and down watching light skitter on her skin, thinking about the colour of things when the sun's on them. She is waiting with the other kids, all the kids in town probably, under the plane trees in the Pioneers' Park. She will not win. Everybody has told her, many times over, that she will not win.

There's laughter all around, and a trumpet is playing over at the grown-ups' celebrations. The tarmac bit in the middle of the park looks like a huge grid. That's where they have prepared the squares for the competition entries.

She has spent many hours practising different drawings, but only in her head, because the box of chalk that Comrade Mantea got for her is not enough for practice on tarmac. She put up a whole circus tent, yellow with green flags, and kept it standing in her head while she did the circus animals. In the classroom, on the bus, in bed at home, she has been non-stop drawing inside her head. The competition judges were there too, and they are always very nice and fair and take a lot of time to look at every line, and they want to speak to her about how she made shade, and they notice when she mixed colours to make orange or purple. After the circus tent, she did an Indian with a hat full of peacock feathers in front of his wigwam, and the kind judges all came again. They pushed the red bike along with them from drawing to drawing, and not one of them had the slightest clue about where the bike would end up before they had looked at every last drawing.

She will not win.

She had a wonderful dream last night. Even after she woke up, for a short while it still felt good, like when you have the right answer to a problem, the one clever thing that will make everybody happy. She dreamed that some other child won, and won a bike, but that she was the runner-up, and they gave her the red of the bike. The red! She could touch it, take it home with her, and this prize, the red of the bike, it was more real than a competition with bad judges and pointless drawings and people who say you don't have a chance.

Finally, the teachers tell their classes to form a line and go up to a long table with a cardboard box. Comrade Cauliflower explained earlier that it's the box with the numbered tickets: *in keeping with the anonymous judging process*, each of the children will have to pull out a ticket and then write it on their drawing slots on the tarmac. When it's her turn to fish out a ticket, Lia closes her eyes.

'Let's see your number, dear,' she hears Cauliflower's voice behind her. The teacher is speaking to Dora. Lia waits, but the teacher doesn't check anyone else's ticket.

Lia heads over to the tarmac and is just about to draw her number in the corner, when Dora shows up in front of her. The girl yanks Lia's ticket out of her hand and gives her another piece of paper instead. 'What's this?' Lia asks.

'Now we'll see,' Dora says. She looks proud and angry, like

she very much wants to say something more. But then there's the starting whistle, and she turns around and walks over to her own slot.

Lia writes the new number in a corner.

She's going to draw a city. A dream city, bright and colourful, with cheerful little houses and a smiling sun. The city has parrots instead of pigeons and a big circus tent. Mother kept telling her to put the circus tent in the background, not right at the front, but Mother doesn't understand it's meant to be a paradise.

Lia doesn't even know when the time passes, she just hears the loud whistle again and realises she has to put down the chalk. She stands up and looks at the drawing. It's feels like magic happened, somehow, and the city that only lived inside her head is now here on the ground. Everyone can see it. She turns around, *look, look*, but all the children are too busy looking at their own drawings.

She wants to lie down and hug her cement square.

All the families are now gathering on the lawn for the award ceremony. Lia spots Mother, Dad and Dani. It's a pity they are too far away to see her drawing. 'It's brilliant!' she mouths at them. She knows what they would say, can see it in Dad's eyes from this distance, but . . . *look at it!* How can she not win?

When the Judging Commission appears, this time for real, Lia forgets to breathe. She watches them go from drawing to drawing and discussing among themselves. They take notes. They stop for a scarily long time in front of some squares. Lia closes her eyes and tries to think of nothing. She tells Mother and Dad again, in her head: yes, Dora is very good at school, but this is drawing. Colours.

When the Commission arrives by her side, she is so nervous that her knees are shaking. She remembers she is supposed to smile. She can hardly see them or hear them, that's how loud her heart beats. She notices as if in a blur that a fat man steps on her drawing. Then suddenly they are gone.

She stands still in the sun. She doesn't want to play around with the others. Something very important is happening, something like the moon and the sun and the stars moving in just the right way so they don't crash, and she stands there, afraid that any wrong step will upset the particular way very important things are supposed to happen.

Finally, the judges come back. The fat man who's the head of the Commission steps on to the podium. He clears his throat.

Number 34. Number 34. Number 34.

'Dear Comrades. On this very special day . . .'

Lia cannot believe how many things the man has to say. He thanks the organisers, the Party, the union leaders, the Dear Leader and his Savant wife, he tells everyone to remember the many sacrifices of the proletariat around the world, the spectacular international results of the country's athletes and pupils, he talks about how pretty their city is and then finally he says:

'. . . it is therefore particularly apposite that the first prize should go to a child who in their artwork glorified this city, its beautiful and clean streets, the homes of its hardworking citizens.'

Lia jumps up and down. *I drew a city! I won!* The nice man goes on.

'The Commission was touched by the chromatic celebration of the town's factory, and by the many . . .'

She stops jumping. What factory? The only big building in her city is the circus tent.

'In other words, the first prize goes to competitor number thirty-four! Come forth, child, tell us your name!' The Head of the Commission turns right and left and adds, 'We don't even know the winner's name, we judged them anonymously.'

Lia's ears are ringing, and she doesn't know where to step and where to look, but somehow she finds her way to the platform. She gives her ticket to the nice judge. He puts his hand on her head. She remembers to smile. She looks out over the audience, but it's too bright to see people's faces.

'Exceptional, absolutely exceptional talent.' The man pauses to catch his breath and wipe his face with the handkerchief. He will ask about her drawing now, Lia thinks, about the colours she used.

'And we have some wonderful news for you. The special prize, the surprise that you've probably heard intriguing rumours about,' he stops to muss her hair, 'is that the Dear Leader and his wife will visit this beautiful town in a few months' time, and that you are the lucky child who will welcome them and be their local guide on their tour here. This is an unheard-of honour!'

Lia keeps smiling. She doesn't understand how the man can speak so much today and not say a word about her bike.

'The winner of the second prize and the recipient of the world-famous Pegasus bicycle is competitor number one hundred and two!' the Head of the Commission then shouts.

The man pushes her aside and puts his arms out to some boy.

'That's my bike,' Lia says. The Head ignores her. Lia pulls his shirt and says it again. She points a finger to her own chest, in case the man can't hear her.

'No, no, you won the big prize.'

He turns away from her.

Lia watches as someone wheels her red bicycle over to this boy, who clambers on to it. It's all happening so fast.

'This, then, marks the end of our festivities,' the Head says. He pinches her cheek. 'Look at these tears of joy!'

Lia wants to argue but she is crying so much she can't breathe. How can this be happening? Her drawing was the best, everyone saw that. She remembers that she did win, it's just that they swapped the prizes. She can't even complain about it. Her thoughts keep going in this awful loop. She's choking on snot.

'We must congratulate this child, and this town, who both must use these coming months to prepare themselves for the great meeting.'

Mother, Lia sees through her tears, has covered her mouth with her hand and is leaning against Dad. Lia escapes that stupid fat man and runs to them. She crashes into Dad's arms.

'They cheated! I won but they gave my bike to someone else!'

'Stop crying,' Dad whispers. 'You, too,' he hisses to Mother.

'This can't be happening,' Mother says. 'It just can't. I refuse to believe it.'

'I know!' Lia cries.

'Victor, we're going to have to pretend she's ill,' Mother

whispers. 'We've got to think of something. This child talking to Ceauşescu?'

'My bike!' Lia sobs.

'Silvia, for God's sake. We'll deal with it later. Look happy,' Dad says, and then he squeezes Lia's shoulder so it hurts, makes her turn around. Cauliflower is coming towards them. The teacher looks furious.

'You stole Dora's number, you . . .' she says.

4

Pitești, March

First, there's a rumour among the police officers about an eerily similar case in the east of the country. Then a week later there's talk of another one. One late afternoon Davidescu plucks up courage and calls his boss's boss; the rumours are confirmed. The police chief comes out of his office and tells them of a priest in a spa town and an elderly hiker in the mountains, both hacked to death like that carpentry teacher at the roadside picnic site.

Constantin sets aside the notebook he had been scribbling in. He can see the alarm in his colleagues' eyes, too, as it dawns on them. Davidescu has not said the words yet, but they are all thinking it. A serial killer.

The body in the ditch was only a beginning. Nobody had even considered that possibility. What else has he missed?

Within a few days several case files arrive in the post from police stations all over the country, and the fax machine starts working non-stop, spewing out awful images. Including the two they already know of, there seem to have been four other similar attacks. And maybe because other regional bosses were quick to weasel out of the assignment, Davidescu has been put in charge of the entire investigation. The police chief swears under his breath when he receives the news over the phone. Walking away, he stumbles on a cord and in revenge kicks the electric radiator so that it topples and slides in under a desk.

The thing lies on its back, reeking of burning plastic, until Maria the secretary dares to stand up and pull out the plug.

Nobody speaks.

'The country needs your superior investigating skills.' Davidescu suddenly turns to Constantin. It's been less than five minutes since the station received the phone call, time in which the boss has been pacing the office with a venomous look in his eye. 'In fact, you've been promoted to chief investigator, right this very minute,' he adds.

What could he have done differently, had he known? Constantin sees before him the gypsy kids he neglected to speak to; the little girl, star-shaped, grinning. He shakes his head, tries to clear his thoughts: the victims are probably unknown to the perpetrator, or only recently known. The notion of motive is different now. The investigation should no longer be looking for a pre-existing conflict. His entire approach has to change.

He starts organising the material. He tells Davidescu right away that he will need two men full-time and unlimited petrol. The police chief nods bitterly, then goes off to make his phone calls.

Constantin orders Vasile to call the four other police stations involved and ask if everything relevant is in the files they just sent. Vasile doesn't understand. 'They might feel more comfortable communicating over the phone rather than leaving a written record,' Constantin explains. 'In case something is . . . sensitive.'

The mood in the station has changed. It is, suddenly and unhappily, no longer an advantageous workplace. Davidescu returns and snaps at everyone, as if they are responsible for this misfortune. He hovers behind their backs and drops ashes on their shoulders. On a regular day the police chief gives the impression of a restive dog, never wants to stand still, but in a crisis he's bristling with menace.

Davidescu stubs out a cigarette on Constantin's desk, looking as if he'd rather stub it out in someone's eye.

Vasile, meanwhile, is oblivious. After every phone call with a remote police station he excitedly reports back to Constantin. The information he has relayed so far has been irrelevant, but he seems to relish the fact that the office is now an intelligence hub of national importance. He whispers over the phone to fellow policemen across the country as though they're trading gossip. *We can hardly believe it. Yes, imagine. Even our coroner is shocked.*

Constantin is torn between being annoyed and hoping that Vasile's chattiness is the right approach for teasing out information.

Davidescu suddenly turns to Vasile. 'You remember the '77 earthquake?'

'Remember it?' Constantin mutters. 'My knees are still

shaking.' He's only half-joking: he had been in Bucharest, on the ground floor of his dorm, and felt liquefied with fear by the earth-roar that preceded the tremors. It had sounded demonic. When the building started swaying it was almost a relief.

'I was talking to our exuberant constable Vasile here,' Davidescu says. 'Our dedicated investigator. Our . . .' the whole office is waiting to hear Davidescu's final insult, '. . . volunteer spirit.'

At long last, Vasile has the good sense to look worried. He opens and closes the phonebook in front of him. He looks at the other faces in the office for support.

'Some new buildings collapsed,' Davidescu goes on. 'Do you know what happened afterwards to their contractors, their engineers?'

Davidescu mimes slicing his throat with his thumb.

Vasile now looks so alarmed that Constantin feels sorry for him. 'We'll catch our man,' he says. 'And it's not like we built shoddy apartment blocks to begin with.'

Davidescu glares at him. 'Tower blocks are built with whatever materials are available. The same goes for this investigation. Ah, you're all stupid cunts.' He stubs out his cigarette and leaves the office.

Constantin leaves work a little early to avoid the worst of the crush on the bus home; Tina has somehow managed to finish their petrol ration already, so he is carless until the end of the month. He successfully squeezes on to the first bus and closes his eyes; they're hurting from deciphering handwritten police reports. His head is still full of the new case files and snippets of possible leads, but he wants to let his mind rest. It's just a short bus trip.

His favourite daydreams are of time-travel, backwards time-travel to be precise. These past weeks, before news of the killings reached them, he had been snatching a free hour here and there and had joined a caravan from Zagora to Timbuktu; there was an article in this year's Almanac about the legendary fifty-two-day Sahara convoys, and those few pages gave enough detail for a journey in his mind, Constantin even tracking his desert fleet's progress across giant orange dunes and black gravel plains on a real-world map. Saharan sand, they say, is cleaner than clean water. His travel companions are swathed in cobalt shawls and speak with their eye-whites. No one has been hacked to death. There is no state and no secret service.

The most satisfying journeys he has dreamed up have been to times and places in which today's world can hardly be imagined. Times and places from where a man might arrive at a different future.

When he gets home he throws his shirt and tie at random over Tina's black half of the wardrobe and collapses on the bed. While he lies dozing, the noises in the other flats blend malignantly with the day's impressions from the office: the old caretaker with his cough on the fourth floor, the footsteps of the obese retired sports teacher in the flat above them, a brief but violent exchange from the unhappy couple on the third floor. And, lurking among them, the killer and his hooks; Constantin has an awful feeling that the ceiling will start dripping blood.

At even intervals he's yanked out of this anxious half-sleep by Tina's piano classes, her students' grim notes. What must the neighbours think of that? He could ask them, he supposes. He could go round and apologise.

'We have to be very careful these days,' he says in the evening. They are in the kitchen, Tina at the stove and Sandu playing on the floor with a toy police car. 'There were some attacks. Nobody should go out after dark. Definitely not alone.'

He doesn't expect an answer; after their many fights, he's gained a good enough understanding of the minefield between him and Tina. He frames his sentences so that they are harmless, his words neither demand nor expect anything. He just needs to communicate the information that she must be careful.

Tina looks at Sandu, then takes a seat cushion from one of the chairs and gives it to the boy.

Constantin hasn't always daydreamed about the past. He tried imagining a change in the present, too, but even in a fantasy setting the challenge is daunting. An entire society putting its foot down at the same time requires, in effect, what? Something like a divine choreographer. What he needs is a point in time when one man, or a small number of people, could in theory have made the necessary difference. In 1908, maybe, or shortly thereafter.

Revolutionary fantasies.

He watches Sandu on the floor rolling his toy car across the columns of the radiator. Tina, at the sink, her back to them, grey roots visible at the top of her head.

Could he have been that past man, capable of that burst of courage, of genuine foresight? At any rate, he likes his chances better than in the present.

* * *

He has shared the new case files with Titus, asked him to have a good look at the other coroners' reports, and now he's in the man's cramped university office, perplexed. Titus is laughing.

'Come on, it's hilarious,' Titus says. Maybe because of the deep grooves on his face, or the million-cigarettes rasp of his voice, with Titus even laughter is a sinister business. 'Don't look at me like that,' the coroner goes on. 'Any stone you turn you find a Securitate mole or a microphone, it's got to the point where they keep carbon copies of our used bog roll, but even they can't find anything on one of the most violent and prolific killers this country has produced. I love it!' He bangs his hand on the desk. 'Can't beat the human spirit.'

Constantin reaches over to a shelf and presses the 'play' button on the small cassette player. Titus always has a tape ready for when they want to discuss sensitive stuff. There's no reason to suspect that his office is bugged, but better safe than sorry.

'Well, this human's spirit feels very defeated,' Constantin says, moving closer to the desk so Titus can hear him over the music.

The murders are geographically dispersed, he explains to Titus, the victims are both men and women, of very different professions and educational backgrounds. They have all been hacked to death.

'I truly hate this piece,' Constantin says, looking at the cassette player. It's always the same cursed song. 'Sounds like band music for deranged trolls.'

'Mad music for a mad world,' Titus shrugs. 'So,' he taps the files. 'You have anything? Witnesses?'

'I wish,' Constantin says.

'Coincidences, anything?'

'Well. The strangest thing is the locations. All over the country,' Constantin says. 'It's a well-travelled murderer.'

'All right, so we have these distances that stick out,' Titus says. 'It should be one of these: a bastard who travels for work, a bastard who travels just to confuse the police, or several bastards across the country working together.'

'I say we rule out the last one,' Constantin waves a hand. 'Can't imagine how they would communicate. How more than one person would keep this secret.'

'Well, then,' Titus says. 'Bastards A or B.'

'Competitions!' Constantin has an idea. 'I'll check with the town halls and see if they were hosting competitions in the same field on those dates. Some kind of professional athlete. Always on the road.'

Titus makes a non-committal face. He opens a pack of cigarettes and lights up.

'You know what's missing here?' he taps the desk. 'You remember – actually you wouldn't, you were not in the force yet – the guy who killed bakers? Just had it in for people making bread.' Titus shrugs. 'There's a reason, always, even if the reason seems deranged to us. Some have it in for women, some are child abusers, some go for young men. The main thing is that the type of victim always tells us something about the killer.'

'This is all over the place,' Constantin says. 'In every possible sense.'

'Ah, but that's what I mean – it can't be, we just haven't

found the connection. Look at it this way: if everyone had it in them to kill, who would they kill? Extrapolate from normal people. Just think of yourself. Wouldn't the identities of your victims tell us a lot about you?'

The music, fittingly, is at that part that sounds as if an ogre is trying to sneak up on a victim.

'Well?' Titus insists.

But Constantin doesn't want to pursue that thought. 'Why not you? Who would Titus kill?' He leans back in the chair.

Titus smiles. 'I'm your very last suspect.' The coroner waves a hand at the gory images pinned to his walls, at the mysterious jars on the top of the fridge. 'I don't feel the slightest need to rush things along. I really – really – know we're all going to die.'

He's back at the station, holding a warm cup of chicory coffee to his chest while once again going through the new material. He is just reaching for a file when the secretary brings a girl to his desk, and leaves her standing awkwardly in front of him. The girl is very small and curvy, dark-skinned with dirty blonde hair. She's in her late teens or even younger, with terrible make-up and wearing the outfit of someone who has tried but failed to remember how to dress respectably.

'Who . . . ?' Constantin says, before it comes to him: the prostitute that Davidescu had insisted on summoning for an interview, well before the case became too serious even for the police chief's perverted sense of humour. He's completely forgotten; everyone has completely forgotten.

Constantin stands up, introduces himself and leads the way

to the interrogation room. He'll go through the motions and let her go.

They sit down.

'So. The night of March the sixteenth.'

The girl has a repertoire of learned expressions, he realises, and currently she's trying to look as though he said something ridiculous. Then she's provocative. He waits for her to compose herself.

'I asked if you remember that night.'

'I didn't do anything,' she says.

'And you are not a suspect. But maybe you saw or heard something?'

She shakes her head.

'Who else was there?'

She steals glances at him and seems increasingly disheartened, as if a plan of hers is going off the rails. Constantin can imagine someone, maybe an older woman, telling her that she should not be afraid of the police, that they can be seduced like all the other men.

He puts a photo of that first victim in front of her. Now that she's here, they need to do this properly; Davidescu could get ideas if she sounds even remotely like she is hiding something. Years ago, when Constantin realised that the police were sometimes asked to produce suspects, evidence be damned, he started collecting the details of deceased individuals who could potentially be framed, and so maybe save someone still alive the ordeal. Even today, if he comes across some dead homeless person, or even better, a deceased criminal, he adds their details to his file. An insane solution to an insane problem.

Titus's mad music rings in his ears.

'Never seen the fellow,' the girl says. 'I'll swear on that.'

'But you remember that night,' he says to the girl, 'the early hours of the morning? We know you were at the lay-by in the Old Forest. Did anyone else maybe see something, mention anything that was odd that night?'

'Well, there was that circus,' the girl says.

Just then, Davidescu opens the door. Constantin can see that he's about to kick them both out, berate him for wasting precious time, but the girl's words stop him in his tracks.

'What fucking circus now?' the police chief says.

'That whole week we had punters from one of them, whaddya call 'em, travelling funfairs. You know? There was tents and stuff set up nearby. We heard they packed up all in a hurry that morning.'

She looks sideways at Davidescu. 'Lots of snotty kids around all the time, we were yelling at them to get the hell away from the trucks. Maybe they saw something.'

A travelling circus. After the girl leaves, Constantin sheepishly expects a reproach from Davidescu for the investigation somehow having missed a whole circus near the murder site. But it doesn't come. The police chief just leaves an open packet of Marlboros on his desk and invites everyone to help themselves. 'We're going to need it,' the chief tells the office.

Back at his desk, Constantin pulls out a map of the area. The travelling circus might have set up camp between the roadside picnic site and the real location of the murder. It would have been one, maximum two kilometres from the murder.

A travelling funfair is always on the road. Strong, athletic men. It fits. A scent, at last.

Snotty kids. Constantin remembers the gypsy girl he didn't think to try to speak to. If the kids belonged to the funfair, they might have seen something.

They might have seen something every single week.

This is the third year. They are sitting in the kitchen, Tina, Sandu and him, around a small cake with seven burning candles and a photo of a little girl shyly looking up at someone outside the frame. It's almost completely dark save for the glow around the cake. Sandu is in Constantin's lap, Tina is across the table. There is no music; in this house there can be no music except work music. It's part of Tina's protest.

It's clear that Sandu has forgotten Alina, but the boy remembers the ritual from last year, and so he is quiet, too. The thin, white birthday candles take about twenty minutes to burn down. He will fall asleep in Constantin's arms.

Nothing else happens, and that is entirely appropriate. It is what death has been like: nothing happens. All roads are permanently blocked. They should have talked about Alina, but he cannot talk about love and loss without hearing, or expecting he'll hear, 'Then why . . . ?' Impossible conversations. They should have consoled each other, but the few times they had sex after that, he felt – and he knows Tina felt the same – that they were doing something altogether different, that there was no joy and pleasure there for them. They are out in the bitter cold, and love is somewhere else.

Sandu whispers a question in his ear. 'No, the cake is not for eating,' Constantin whispers back.

Even with Sandu, sometimes he feels he is trying to stretch himself past the roadblock to guide the boy onwards, but he is not walking with him. He is just doing his best to hold his hand and speak to him for as long as he can.

'We've got to warn the public,' Constantin says in the office the next morning.

'A warning, now?' Davidescu asks.

'Something, I don't know. That there's a dangerous killer on the loose.'

'We're in America all of a sudden. Bang, bang!' Davidescu mimes two-handed revolver shooting, complete with noises. Then, he points a finger at Constantin. 'Why aren't you out there chasing clowns?'

Constantin explains that he and Vasile are doing their best to track down the funfair; the last update is that they were in a town in the north, but that was a week ago and they have moved on. There's no way of locating them other than calling around town halls and seeing if they issued a funfair permit.

'But seriously, it's unconscionable,' Constantin insists. He looks around the office. 'We all warned our families. We have to warn everyone.'

Davidescu swears loudly. 'You're not thinking. That kind of announcement will cause panic. It'll make us look bad, the entire state apparatus: police, government . . . And we won't get anything in return for our troubles. What the hell can we tell people? We can't give anyone a single piece of advice that might help them stay alive.'

Constantin gets it; Davidescu is worried that making it public will increase the pressure on the station to catch the killer. 'It doesn't have to be like that,' Constantin says. 'The more careful people are, the fewer murders, the less trouble for us.'

'Careful of what?' Davidescu says. 'Some of these people died in their homes.'

'To lock the doors. Not to trust strangers.'

Davidescu picks up one of the new case files and starts reading out loud. 'The assailant forced the door open, possibly by kicking it in.' The police chief slams the file on the table. 'You've got no useful advice to offer the public. Panic, distrust of the police, and the politically unacceptable premise that we've produced one of those capitalist serial killers.'

'There are lots of bear attacks where I'm from,' Vasile says. 'Every winter some poor bastard gets done in. I never understood, what are bears even doing out and about in winter?'

Davidescu was about to shout something else; now he's frowning at Vasile. 'Are you still with us? Do we need to rewind a cassette somewhere?'

'I mean,' Vasile stutters, 'why don't we say it's a bear?'

Davidescu's frown lifts slowly. 'Say it's a bear,' he repeats.

Constantin puts his head in his hands.

'I think it's a very good idea,' Vasile says.

'We give them the location of the attacks. Yes.' Davidescu has turned around, goes on speaking as if to himself. 'Bears are fucking nasty, people will take the threat seriously. We can make sure the public gets told of an attack, the location and all that as soon as we hear of it. Best of all – a rabid bear is not just the police's remit. The public will blame the army and the forestry service too.'

He turns to Constantin. 'If you have a single piece of information to add that would help someone stay safe, by all means, enlighten us. Come on. Speak now or forever hold your peace.'

Can it really be different elsewhere, Constantin thinks? In other countries and other times. Could things be so different? Maybe this is it, that's all there is on offer here, and really he should be dreaming of travelling in outer space. He imagines a lone rocket, floating happily among the stars. No lies, no past mistakes to disentangle. Pure hope of kind new worlds.

They have chicken claw soup for supper. Sandu loves the claws, makes loud noises as he sucks on the cartilage, but still Constantin can't look Tina in the eye. She thinks chicken claws are not what other cops' children eat. It's poor Sandu, again, who saves him from the dinner table. 'Fairy-tale night, Daddy!'

They settle into the armchair.

'Guess what?' Constantin says. He waves the notebook at Sandu. 'Tonight we really have a prince. Once upon a time, in a mountainous land far away, a little boy was born to the King and a Queen, and the court started preparing for a great celebration. Invitations were sent to the entire nobility of the country, to neighbouring rulers, and to the three famous witches of the land, who since memory began had bestowed magic gifts on every royal offspring.

'The celebrations started, and everyone had a merry time for three days and three nights. At the end of the feasts, it was time for the witches to reveal their gifts. The first one stepped forward and laid down a golden purse next to the baby. "As soon as it's emptied, this purse shall fill anew with ducats." The audience gasped and clapped, and the parents were very satisfied with this gift of unending riches.

'The second one stepped forward and put a little flask next to the boy. "The liquid in this flask shall heal any wound, cure any illness, and render powerless any poison."

'The Queen cried with joy. Good health and riches, what more could they have wished for their child? And there was yet one more gift.

'However, when the third witch was due to speak, no one stepped forward. The servants went and looked for her in her chamber, but they couldn't find her. Soon it became apparent that mistakes had been made, lists of invitees copied wrong, and no one had actually invited the third witch. The King and Queen were very upset because the boy would now be deprived of a third magic gift.

'The party continued for a little while longer, and then the Queen signalled to the women to take the boy to his chamber and put him to bed. The wet nurse picked up the boy, and gave a shriek. She almost dropped the child.'

Constantin pauses. A bear! How had it even come up in conversation? He frowns, struggles to understand Davidescu's thinking. 'Makes no sense. The public will still panic – it's a goddamn homicidal bear,' he mutters.

'Daddy?' Sandu says, tugs at the notebook.

'Where was I? Yes – it turned out the poor baby had grown a tail. A long, thin tail stuck out from under his tunic, it even wagged a little as the boy had woken up. Everyone in the palace heard an evil laughter, and they knew that this tail was the witch's revenge for being forgotten.

'The Queen cried for weeks on end. They consulted with doctors: could they cut off the tail? But no doctor dared operate on a bewitched tail.

'The boy grew up to be shy and withdrawn. As soon as he was able to, he cut off the tail by himself. He endured horrible pain, only for the thing to grow back. The boy hated the tail, and because the tail was attached to him, he hated himself. In his teens now, there were girls he liked, but he was so ashamed of his tail that he couldn't believe that anyone liked him.

'What about the other gifts? Well. The magic purse was given to the boy when he was fifteen, and from then on he used it sparingly. But there was hardly a month when someone didn't try to steal it. Everyone wanted his purse, and was prepared to kill him for it.

'He was a healthy young man, and would probably have hardly ever needed the magic potion, were it not for all the attempts on his life brought about by the magic purse. By his twenty-fifth year, he had finished the magic potion. He had the wisdom to see that without the potion and with the purse, his days were numbered, and so he organised a public ceremony. He showed everyone that it was indeed the magic purse, by emptying it over and over again, and then he threw the purse into the hot spring, where it disappeared with a golden burst of sprinkle. After that day he lived in bitterness, aggrieved about his tail and the uselessness of the two allegedly fabulous gifts he had been given.

'One day the Prince, now King, travelled with his retinue across snowy mountains. They were caught in an avalanche, and the King was swallowed up by the snow. Once the mountain had settled, the servants started searching for the King. But the whole expanse was white, and they could see no sign of anyone, until an eagle-eyed archer spotted something sticking out of the snow some distance away. They ran to the spot, and saw it was the tip of the King's tail. They dug him up, and were very grateful to see that he was only unconscious.

'When the King came to his senses, and was told how he was rescued, he had what we call an epiphany. From then on he was happy and content, and lived at peace with his tail. And the tail thrived, too – it was no longer naked and thin, like a rat's tail, but healthy and bushy, more like a fox's tail. The King learned to use it to keep him warm in winter, and to shield his eyes on bright nights.'

Sandu claps his hands. 'I want a tail!'

'You liked this one?'

The boy nods. He's resting his small hand on the notebook, as though he wants to touch the story.

Sometimes Constantin catches himself with the absurd hope that Sandu will be clever enough not to need any guidance from him: will know when to be quiet, when to speak and even when to lie without any further assistance. How do children learn to function in this world? Whenever he imagines Sandu performing any of the million grown-up lies or humiliating silences that will be necessary for staying out of trouble, he feels crushed.

Constantin kisses the top of the boy's head. 'Hats bad, tails good. I'll try to remember.'

After he puts Sandu to bed, he goes to the kitchen and sits in the dark. Apart from anything else, he would very much like to smoke again; they go together well, thinking and smoking. It annoys him that it was Davidescu's perverse and seemingly useless impulse that led to the police learning about the circus.

5

Sighișoara, May

It's evening, and they're all in front of the TV. Dad came back the day before from a work trip. He looked tired and thin, and almost fell over when Lia and Dani jumped on him at the door. He went straight to sleep and only woke up a few hours ago because he was hungry. They all had fried eggs, and Mother forgot to turn Lia's egg, but Lia was good and didn't say anything and ate it runny like that. Mother kept stroking Dad's face. Dad took Mother's hand and said, 'I hope we can forget about this whole thing now. Just forget it.'

Lia has her notebook in her lap. She has been working on an inventory of every colourful thing in the world. The word *inventory* is sometimes written on the front doors of shops when they are closed. It's a very good word. Mother explained it means making a list of what you have, so you don't get robbed without knowing it.

Right now she is writing down all the flowers that are in the garden in front of the blocks. There are two sunflowers, and in the narrow flower bed at one end there are blue, violet, yellow and orange pansies. Here and there are poppies. Poppies are pretty little weaklings who don't even survive the trip up the stairs to a vase; she tried several times even though the garden is forbidden to children. It's protected by the most annoying neighbours and by a hedge with bunches of white, cloudy berries that make a 'plop' sound when you step on them. If this weren't such an important inventory she would put the berries in it, too. They're plain white but that plop they make is lots of fun.

Mother has been watching the TV with her hand over her mouth. The bad bear is on the news. 'Another one, can you believe it?' she whispers. 'Poor, poor people.'

'Two more attacks while I was away? But – how can they be so far from the first one?' Dad says. 'I don't get it.'

As on other bear nights, the newsman points his stick at a map that has a cross for the last attack. Then they show a sad-looking bear walking in circles. Lia feels sorry for the bear in his filthy cage, especially since Mother explained that this is not the actual bad bear.

'You know what I was thinking?' Mother says. 'That mon-ster – our monster – he was found butchered in his garage on the outskirts of town, early in the morning. Couldn't it have been . . . ?'

The last weeks have been strange. The bear is all anyone speaks about. A boy in 3B who has a policeman uncle in another town bragged that he's seen a photograph of one of the dead people. The boy doesn't even have this photograph, but during breaks all the children gather around him begging to hear the story again. Another classmate has completely stopped going out, and everyone is waiting for the police to go to his house and force his parents to let him come to school.

'So what?' Dad says.

'Well, if it was this cursed bear,' Mother says, 'then maybe they could finally leave us alone.'

Dad sighs. 'They already know it wasn't me. I told you, they were going to drop me from the investigation altogether before . . .' Dad turns to look at Lia. He waves a hand. 'Never mind that now.'

'But that's crazy,' Mother says. 'It was just a silly competition. And I bet a chief prosecutor's daughter doesn't even need some excuse of a prize if her parents really want her to meet Ceaușescu.'

'Silvia. They need to pin it on someone,' Dad says. 'Guilty or not. We just have to hope . . . Shh,' he says, and points at the TV.

In a disappointed voice, the newsman is chiding the people who cannot bring themselves to be a little more careful despite all the warnings.

'But really, how are they not catching it?' Mother asks Dad. 'How is it possible? It's an animal.'

'Maybe it's several?' Dad speaks. 'Hence the distances.'

Lia hasn't told them about the classmate who's no longer allowed to come to school. They'll get ideas. Mother has already forbidden her to go beyond the courtyard of the two blocks. Even the car park where the boys play football is forbidden.

'Several rabid bears?' Mother says in a disbelieving voice.

'Can't be rabid,' Dad says. 'It's too clever. Besides, it would have been dead from rabies by now.'

'What do you think it wants? I mean, really, how many people can one bear eat?' Mother puts a hand on her stomach and makes a grimace as if she's in pain.

'The army and the police are assisting the forestry service,' the newsman says, 'and the Comrade President himself is monitoring the situation closely. The beast will be caught.'

Comrade President.

'It was the worst prize ever,' Lia says. 'I don't want it, and everybody is angry at me that I won. I hate it.'

That's the other thing everyone's talking about. They have even bought her a calendar. Dad circled the National Day some three months from now, and hung the calendar in the kitchen over the washing machine. Tuesdays and Fridays she has to go to 'special classes', and Mother makes her wear an outfit called the 'parade uniform': an ugly plasticky dress that crackles and makes her hair stand on end when she pulls it on and off. There are new poems she has to learn, and 'forms of address'.

Mother shakes her head. 'How can anyone seriously think we are desperate for this child to chit-chat with Ceaușescu?'

'Lia. You know you can't talk like that,' Dad says.

Suddenly, Mother slaps the armrests. 'But for the love of God,' she says, 'who in his right mind thinks he can outrun a bear?'

The newsman has been saying that citizens should 'exercise utmost caution, and not put themselves in the situation where they might need to escape the beast'.

'A bear is faster than a horse over short distances,' Dad says quietly, nodding at the screen. 'He'll catch any of us.'

Lia remembers she had a question. 'Dad, is it true they have colour TV in Germany?'

Ewald, in her class, who has a *Tante* and *Onkel* in Germany who send him beautiful things like his pencil case that is the envy of the whole school, this boy Ewald has told everyone that in Germany the TV is chock-full of colours.

Dad doesn't say anything. Lia hears Mother huffing next to him.

'Well, is it?' Lia says.

'I think so,' Dad says. 'But colour TV is bad for your eyes, that's why we don't have it here.'

'Shhh!' Mother says, her eyes still on the news.

'The public can rest assured that authorities will catch the bear and put an end to the beast's reign of terror.' The newsman closes the seven o'clock news the same way he does every time there's an attack. 'In the meantime, citizens must go about their duties with added caution and responsibility.'

She gets back to the inventory. There isn't much time. The other day when Mother and Dad were at work Lia took the box of Christmas baubles down from the top of the wardrobe, to properly count them and put them in her World Inventory, and she noticed that there's a difference even between the baubles from three to four years ago and the ones they bought last year. It's happening very fast.

There's another important word, *extinct*, that's in Grandpa's atlas, a word written next to pictures of dinosaurs, dodos and mammoths. If nobody puts a stop to this, that's what it will be like. A picture of the sun in a big old book with the note, 'Last known specimen of yellow.'

The next day Lia sneaks over to the neighbouring block. She walks up to the second floor, first making sure that no neighbours are on the landing to rat on her to Mother. Sometimes she walks right past Comrade Mantea's door and goes up to the next floor, to trick any nosybodies watching through the peephole. Sometimes she does this twice or three times, goes up and down and up again, to bore the nosybodies to death in case they haven't been tricked.

She knocks on his door. He cracks it open and squints at her. 'What?'

'I want to ask you something.'

In the kitchen, Comrade Mantea points to the chair at the other end of the table and plonks a bowl of sunflower seeds in front of her.

They look at one another. She wonders if she will get the good Comrade Mantea or the bad one. Sometimes he's so drunk that he doesn't reply when she says hello to him in the street. Right now, in a worn bathrobe and pyjama bottoms, unshaven, Comrade Mantea just looks old. The smell of drink, it's always there.

'So. What's up, kid?'

'Do you know they are stealing the colours?'

Comrade Mantea frowns. 'What's with this colour obsession? Jesus, kid. Jump rope. Play ball. Break windows. But leave the damn colours alone. Here, have a drink.'

She reaches for the smelly, full glass that he has pushed in front of her. He lets out a sound that is half-growl and half-laughter and snatches the glass back. She giggles.

The phone rings just then. She sits back, waiting for Comrade Mantea to answer. But he doesn't even get up. He just glares at the white telephone on the fridge. It rings and rings and Comrade Mantea just stares at it. She has never seen anyone not answer the phone.

'Let him think I'm dead,' he mutters after it stops ringing.

Then he turns cheerful and pats her on the head. 'Want to play?' he asks. He reaches across the kitchen and picks up a matchstick box from the side of the stove.

He taught her this game. You perch the matchstick box flat on the edge of a table, leaving half of it to jut out. The idea is to then flip the box from beneath with your thumbnail so that it jumps up and lands on the table. There are three possible positions and it has to spin at least once for the landing to count. You get no points at all if it lands flat.

'Do you think he'll send the police to check on me?' Comrade Mantea chuckles. He prepares his first flip. He looks up at Lia, quickly, like she has contradicted him. 'He's done that before, you know! When I didn't answer the phone.'

His matchbox lands flat on its belly.

Lia tells him her terrible news. 'They're making me take special preparation classes after school, with Comrade Cauliflower.' Mother also said that everything else depends on how the teacher likes 'her progress'. They might ban cartoons, reading, outdoor playtime. The colouring.

'It's a disaster,' she says.

Comrade Mantea shakes his head. 'The last time he came to

see me, it's – what's it now, May? Must have been December. My own son. But he sends food! Oh yes! Kilos of it!' Comrade Mantea suddenly waves his arms. 'Shanks of lamb and whole legs of pork! Smoked trout, pike roe salad and liver pâté – will you believe it, I'm eating food from the Party's own restaurants! Jars of pickled cauliflower, of peppers, of pickled everything. Salami, hot dogs, smoked *Kaiserfleisch*. Eat, eat, eat. Eat . . . Your . . . Son!'

These last words he almost shouted. He points at the freezer. 'Must be the only well-stocked freezer on our damn street.' His eyes light up again. 'Actually – aren't you hungry? Here!'

He gets on his knees beside the freezer and starts taking out tightly wrapped parcels from the drawers. He squints at each of them before throwing them on the floor. 'It says on them what they are. Look – this says veal, take it.'

'I'm not hungry,' she says.

Dani and Dad probably are, but where will she tell them she got it from? She isn't even allowed to talk to Comrade Mantea. *Veal steak: dropped from the sky.*

Comrade Mantea makes a sad gesture at the parcels on the floor. 'Or maybe I'll cook something next time. Then you can eat here.'

'There's even a special uniform,' Lia goes on. 'And all this for the stupid Dear Leader meeting,' she tells him.

'Ah yes.' Comrade Mantea leans on a chair to get back up. He chuckles. 'Still can't believe they chose Anarcho-Thumbelina here to meet Ceauşescu. Crazy.'

She nods. 'It's a rotten prize. And rotten special classes.'

'That's it, scram,' he says. 'I need a nap before going out.'

He's always going out in the evening. *Drink, it's a poison,* Mother says and shakes her head when she sees Comrade Mantea on his way to the workers' bar.

'You'll still go out at night even if the bear comes to our county?' she asks. 'Mother says we mustn't go far from home. It's dangerous.'

'There's no bear, kid.'

'The bear is always on the news,' she says quietly. 'Maybe even tonight.'

Comrade Mantea gets up then and opens the door to the other room. He goes over to the sofa and the small table standing next to it, grabs the white sheet covering the table and pulls it off to show . . . a TV. The small table is really a television.

'Excellent height for resting my tea on when I sit here and read. It also doubles as a footrest. The possibilities are infinite!' He laughs.

A TV as a table. Lia is amazed.

'Does it work?' she asks.

'I wouldn't know. It worked back in the day. Poured endless rubbish into my ear. I haven't turned it on for years. That's it, kid.' He leads her out of the room and back into the kitchen.

'So, there's no bear,' he says again. 'This Communist Paradise of ours, you know what I mean?'

Not really. When she was still trying to decide what to draw, Lia asked Mother and Dad what 'Communist Paradise' actually means, if it's about heaven and angels, and Dad said, 'No, it's just a metaphor. It's when we say that something is something else, but only because the two things have some quality in common, not because they really are the same.' Lia thought it all sounded very much like the metaphors she's been telling all her life, but which Dad and Mother have always called 'disgusting, filthy lies'.

'Hey, you.' Comrade Mantea snaps his fingers at her. 'Listen. Do we have criminals?'

'The criminals are in the West,' she says.

'Exactly, that's what they keep telling us. A perfect society like ours doesn't have criminals. Except, of course it does. All societies have criminals. Some, like the ones in power . . .' he looks at her and waves a hand. 'Never mind those now. There are common criminals, there is theft. There is murder. And sometimes there is something like this, a killer who is monstrous, who just keeps killing until they stop him.'

He looks at her, waits for her to say something. She doesn't think she has understood.

'There is a killer, a human killer,' Comrade Mantea says slowly. 'No bear.'

'But who is the bear in the cage, then?'

'What are you talking about?'

'You know, the bear. The one they are showing every time they talk about the attacks.'

'Does it matter? It's just some bear.'

She tries to rearrange everything inside her head. There's so much of it.

'The sad thing is . . .' Comrade Mantea pokes her with a finger. 'Hey, you – look at me! You want to hear what the sad thing is?'

'Yes.'

'This poor fellow on the news, or whoever it was who

decided to broadcast the story with the bear, he has probably taken a big risk with this idea. Our leadership didn't want it reported that we have a serial killer, so someone must have come up with the idea of blaming it on an animal. That way at least they can warn people in the region of the murders to stay indoors. This fellow is actually a hero. Do you understand this word, kid? Heroic?'

'Like, in the books? Hercules?'

'Yes. Except,' he says, and pretends to be holding something tiny between his finger and thumb, 'ours are minuscule heroes. Minuscule acts. That's all we do. Almost completely useless acts of tiny heroic resistance. There now, scram.'

In bed that night Lia thinks about their rotten TV that pours black-and-white rubbish into their ears. Maybe there is some way of colouring it. Dad could open it at the back, the way he's always opening up the car and doing things to its engine. She imagines the TV engine, and Dad with a fuel canister pouring a rainbow petrol down the TV's back. She imagines the colour rising in the TV from the bottom up, just like water in a glass. The Dear Leader, looking up in surprise at the colour around him—

Lia immediately sits up in the dark. But of course. Who is the one person who can do something about the missing colours? It's so obvious. She just has to let the Dear Leader know. This is better than anything Mother and Dad can do, better than a colour TV.

'Dani!' she whispers, but Dani is fast asleep. Lia looks down at her belly, where suddenly there's an excited rumble. Belly feelings are always true.

★　　★　　★

The next time she goes to visit Comrade Mantea she walks straight into a block meeting on the ground floor. They all stare at her – the neighbours standing in front of their doors, or leaning on the bannister higher up along the landing. Pensioners in housecoats, men in slippers. The women must have left their pots cooking; it smells of onions.

'You heard them. Should we maybe have a neighbourhood watch?'

It's the block administrator speaking.

She sneaks past the grown-ups and sits down on a step; she can't go in to Comrade Mantea's now. Some of these nosy-bodies will have nothing better to do than run straight to Mother and rat on her.

'How on earth will a neighbourhood watch help? I mean, it's not like the beast is afraid of people. Will the watchers have guns? No. So what are these neighbourhood watchers supposed to be, other than bear snack?'

Lia giggles, but she's the only one. She wishes Comrade Mantea were out here, to explain how there's no bear. A talk between him and the neighbours would help her understand better.

'At least it's nowhere near here,' a woman sighs.

'Yeah, and who do you think butchered our neighbour back in March?' a man says. 'I know from his cousin the police now think it was the bear.'

'But, have you noticed? It never attacks children,' another woman says.

'That's wonderful for the dear little children,' the bear-snack man says, 'but I would also rather not be mauled to death.'

They go on for at least half an hour. She has noticed there's a special bear-talking voice that the grown-ups have. She doesn't like it one bit. The voices have changed since the first attacks happened, when everyone was still saying it was just one time, just terrible bad luck that had struck some poor forestry workers. She can't really explain the difference. But when Mother and Dad or neighbours talk about the bear now, it makes her upset even if she isn't paying attention to their actual words. They sound like they are little, too, like they are hoping there's someone more grown-up than them who will keep them safe.

Her bottom hurts from the concrete by the time the neighbours finally say their goodbyes and go into their flats.

'You missed a block meeting,' she says to Comrade Mantea when he opens the door.

'I've missed them all since '75,' he says, turning away from her. 'They'll have to chain me to the postboxes if I'm to sit through one.'

They go to the kitchen. He is unshaven, in that ancient bathrobe, and his hair looks greasy and messy. The kitchen is full of unwashed dishes and overflowing ashtrays. It smells dirty. She likes it very much that you never know what's going to happen with Comrade Mantea.

'You know what's funny about this bear thing?' Comrade Mantea says. 'Everybody is suddenly armed to the teeth, and the authorities are oblivious. Grandmas with bread knives in their purses, men carrying axes to work! These people now just need a particular idea to cross their mind. Re-vo-lu-tion!'

He picks up a dishcloth and tries to clear some space at the table. He plonks a cup lined with old grime in front of her;

fills it with mineral water. Then he goes, 'Ah!', and takes a pot out of the fridge, puts it on the stove.

'It's probably disgusting. My wife, before she died, she left me a notebook with her best recipes. But who can bear to look at her handwriting?' He turns something over in the pot. 'So this is not one of her best recipes.'

'Cauliflower doesn't like my handwriting either,' Lia says.

'That's not what I mean, kid. Mona's writing was beautiful.'

'It smells nice,' she says. It really does.

Comrade Mantea puts it all on a plate in front of her and watches her eat, looking pleased. 'If your parents weren't such uptight little bolsheviks I could send food over for the whole family.'

She nods, her mouth too full. Dani would love this, that's for sure.

When she has licked the plate clean, she remembers she has been meaning to tell him about her brilliant idea. But after the block meeting she has the bear on her mind. Or the bad man. It's confusing to think about them both. When she isn't with Comrade Mantea, she thinks about the bear, and when she's with him, she remembers it's meant to be a bad man.

She closes one eye, and then the other, trying to make proper room for both of them in her head.

Comrade Mantea looks at her. 'What did they do to you, kid?'

The doorbell rings then. They both go quiet.

Another ring.

'Is this about that stupid block meeting?' he whispers to her. 'The daft buggers took some initiative, they want the neighbourhood to go catch Baloo?'

She giggles.

He keeps staring at the hallway. Another ring. It occurs to her then that maybe it's Mother, and she feels her knees go soft. Someone must have seen her enter the flat.

'Come on, I've got a key anyway.' They hear a man's voice on the outside.

Lia is so relieved she whistles.

Comrade Mantea points at the bedroom door. 'Stay there!' he whispers.

She closes the door behind her and looks through the key-hole. Comrade Mantea returns to the kitchen, followed by a man who is about Dad's age. He sits in the chair that Lia has been sitting in. He drops the canvas bag that he's brought with him and pushes it under the table with his foot, towards Comrade Mantea. Then he crosses his legs and looks around the kitchen.

'I can't bring back Mum, but I could definitely send someone to help you keep the place clean.'

'Pretty much the last thing I want to hear is what you can and cannot do,' Comrade Mantea says.

'Is this,' the man waves a hand at the kitchen, 'your idea of rebellion?'

'None of anyone's damn business.'

The man just sits and looks at Comrade Mantea. 'You're still drinking,' he eventually says. 'I thought we talked about that.'

'Well, you're still an apparatchik.'

The man laughs. 'Let's think about it. Your drinking helps no one. But me being what you call an apparatchik helps feed you, Aunt Maria, my useless cousin . . .' With his foot, the man nudges the canvas bag closer to Comrade Mantea. 'If we're going to keep score.'

Why is Comrade Mantea allowing the man to speak to him like this? Lia can't see her friend through the keyhole, only this other proud man that she doesn't like one bit.

'I don't understand what's happened to you,' Comrade Mantea says.

'Again? Dad. I'm so fed up with this.'

Dad?

'What did you ever do? You just never this and never that. But it takes more of a man to fight for a place at the table than to sit here into all eternity and drink and whine.'

'You know I had you and your mother to worry about.'

This man is Comrade Mantea's son?

'You keep telling yourself that,' the man says. 'How convenient.'

'I don't even get why you keep coming. Just leave me alone.'

'You're old. Someday you'll realise I'm all you have left. That it's too late to be an armchair revolutionary. You've got grandchildren, act like it! Ask me about them, come and visit, for fuck's sake!'

At the swearword, Lia recoils from the keyhole and bumps into a chair.

'What was that?' she hears from the kitchen.

'Never mind,' Comrade Mantea says. He sounds exhausted.

'What's with the secretiveness? It's great if you have a woman. Though she needs to work on her housekeeping skills.'

'Oh, go to hell.'

A moment's silence, then Lia hears the front door.

Carefully, she opens the door to the kitchen. Comrade Mantea is sitting at the table, staring into thin air.

Lia doesn't know what to say. In the end she asks, 'Where does your son live?'

'My son isn't the problem, kid.'

She doesn't believe this. Maybe Comrade Mantea is embarrassed she heard his son talk to him like that.

'I am the problem,' Comrade Mantea says.

'The drinking?' she dares. Drinking is one of the things that's not mentioned in public, especially to people who do the drinking.

Comrade Mantea waves an arm. 'That? No.'

They sit some more. She stares at the kitchen clock that's stuck at eight o'clock.

'Maybe you'll do better, kid. Though I doubt they'll let you.'

'Let me?'

Comrade Mantea sighs. 'It's like a tunnel, somehow, and when you come out at the other end you realise you're not yourself any more.' He looks at her as though he has been making sense. 'You don't even know it, that you're in that tunnel.'

'Can we play a round?' she says.

'Oh, I don't know how to put it. It would be great, kid, it would be wonderful, if you could find a way of growing up so that you like yourself, and like your life, and where you are in the greater scheme of things.'

She smacks her forehead. But of course: her brilliant idea, it can help Comrade Mantea too.

'I have a plan!' she says. 'When I meet the Dear Leader, I'm going to ask him if he can do something about the colours. I'll tell him that everyone is sad and angry because bad people are stealing the colours.'

She waits for Comrade Mantea's face to change, for him to realise the importance of what she just said.

He still looks sad. 'Ah yes, I keep forgetting. Your big meeting.'

'And if you want, I can ask something for you as well! You just have to think what you want from him.'

At first, she thinks that Comrade Mantea is laughing; he is heaving and has covered his face with his hands. But no. She sinks in her chair.

'Go home,' he says through his sobs.

It's only hours later, when she's in bed, that she comes up with the right thing to say to Comrade Mantea to make him feel better. It's something all grown-ups need telling, especially Mother and Dad: they worry too much for people who are good. She will have to explain that she doesn't mean 'good' as in 'do-your-homework good', but the good of fairy tales, of parents who take care of their children, of nice, friendly neighbours. Of people who want more colour. It's as if they don't know that everything always ends well for the good ones.

Comrade Mantea's sadness stays with her for days. He had been crying, and men never cry. She can't ask Mother and Dad about it, but at school she tries to make sense of it together with Ewald. It is difficult, solving grown-ups' problems.

'Somebody must have died. Old people are sad because other old people die,' Ewald says, and refuses to understand that Comrade Mantea's sadness was about being lost in a tunnel. Or that he isn't that kind of old.

'They're always going to funerals,' Ewald insists.

She remembers then that she has another problem.

'You have very nice fingernails,' she bursts out to Ewald. They are pink, naturally, beautiful pink, the best fingernails ever except for the one time that Mother painted hers red. Ewald is still staring at his fingers, confused, when she adds, 'Can I borrow your pencil case?' He shouldn't be able to say no after that compliment. 'Please? Just for today. To explain to my parents about Germany.'

Mother and Dad will have to believe her about colourful Germany if they see the pencil case themselves.

The boy puts his hands with their pretty fingernails in his pockets, but he lets her have the pencil case, and when Mother and Dad are together in front of the TV that evening Lia shows it to them.

'They have things like this in Germany,' she says. She shows Mother and Dad the glossy blue lid, how the pencil case opens and closes, the greedy smack of the magnet. The beautiful perfumed erasers and felt-tips, in five colours. She lifts the pencil case to their noses so they can smell it.

Mother rolls her eyes.

Lia feels like a magician who's boring the audience. Maybe they don't understand. 'We should go there on holiday,' she says, 'not to Kishinev.'

'Germany! Can you believe . . . ?' Mother says to Dad. She's angry again. 'It doesn't matter where the damn thing is from!' She grabs Lia's arm and takes the pencil case from her.

'Silvia,' Dad says.

Mother ignores him. 'If I hear another word about Germany, you'll have a worse spanking than you can imagine!'

'The authorities have identified a tenth victim,' the newsman says on the TV.

'Lucky bastard!' Mother bursts out. She sinks into the sofa.

'Don't talk like that,' Dad says to Mother. Then he pats Lia's head. 'Germany. Sure, and we'll go to the USA too.'

'It's not funny,' Mother says. 'What if she starts telling people she wants to go to Germany?'

'Didn't you hear, she actually intends to come back here afterwards? *A holiday*. They'll give our girl a medal.'

Dad is in that mood when he just wants to laugh.

'Victor. Be serious.'

'It is still illegal to shoot bears without a hunting licence and corresponding permissions.' In his sad, disappointed voice, the newsman is now telling people to report bear sightings, and not to try to shoot the animal themselves. Someone, in a night-time panic, has even shot a poor dog. 'And remember, this bear has to date eluded the efforts of our mighty army. One man with a shotgun will not bring it down. Follow our updates of the bear's location and practise maximum caution.'

It's been weeks now since Comrade Mantea has told her the secret about the bear, but no one else seems to have figured it out.

'God forgive me,' Mother says, 'but between this bear and our daughter I'm going insane.'

In bed that night, Lia practises the talk that she will have with the Dear Leader. She sees herself in the middle of the National Day parade, bunting on the street and trumpets, patiently explaining the colour problem. It's not the best time to do so, because for the National Day party they bring out what little colour there is – the flags, the uniforms, the golden brass instruments. But the Dear Leader will of course understand what she means; he's not always in the middle of a National Day Parade. And if he tries to say that colour is expensive – grown-ups always say things are expensive – she can tell him about her colour shop idea. Put all the expensive colourful things in one special colour shop, and let the people who like them so much pay for it. That would be fair.

It's finally a good day, she can tell from the doorway. Comrade Mantea smells of drink and has a ruddy nose. His eyes are cheerful and he tousles her hair when he opens the door.

'My most distinguished visitor!' He shows her into the kitchen with a bow.

She climbs on to her usual chair and asks if they can play the matchbox game. He rubs his hands together and grabs the box.

'Have you been practising?' he says. 'I'll have to go on a high-altitude matchbox training camp to keep up with you.'

She giggles.

'How are the preparations going? For your big meeting?'

She tells him how boring it all is. The two songs she has to learn, and the three poems. And the other stuff, about not being allowed to say anything other than the words Comrade Cauliflower puts in her mouth. 'Like I'm one of those stupid wind-up chickens,' she grumbles. 'You know, the toys?'

Comrade Mantea nods. 'But! They didn't say anything about gifts, did they?'

Gifts?

'I was thinking,' he goes on, 'we should prepare a surprise gift for the Dear Leader.'

She finds herself with her mouth open in astonishment. A secret surprise, what a brilliant idea. She's ashamed she hasn't thought of it herself.

'You like this idea, I can tell.'

She almost nods her head off.

'But it's important that no one else knows about it. Especially that brassica teacher of yours. Or your parents. You know how it is – as soon as you mention a good idea, they forbid it. We've got to keep this one quiet.'

At that point, Comrade Mantea strikes the underside of the matchbox with his thumb. The box flies nearly up to the kitchen lamp. It lands with a thud on its belly.

'Zero points!' She snatches the matchbox from him. 'And then we tell him about the colours. He's the only one who can help.'

'Well, he'll be in an excellent mood after receiving his gift.'

Lia agrees. It's the perfect plan.

'But,' Comrade Mantea says, 'you know what would be useful? To find out more about the exact schedule for the day. Where will you meet the Dear Leader? At what time? For how long? Ask your teacher. Just say it is so you can prepare better.'

She nods.

'Think of it as a super-important spying mission. You have

to obtain information by stealth, without being compromised. You'll have to use your brain, kid. You'll have to be brave.'

He explains the new word and then she gives Comrade Mantea a proper thrashing at the matchbox game. He pretends to be dejected, to kick her out of his flat before she has had the meatballs and tomato sauce that he promised her.

After she's eaten, he stops her in the doorway and turns her around. He puts his hands on her shoulders and bows down until his eyes are level with hers. He isn't cheerful any more.

'I would never let anything bad happen to you, do you understand? Everything I'm planning is so that you can have a decent future. It pains me to think of the kind of soulless apparatchik they'll make of you if we let them.'

6

Copşa Mică and Piteşti, May

Constantin has tracked down the travelling funfair to a small town in the middle of the country, and now he and Vasile are in the police car, on their way there. He is hopeful. It's been suspiciously difficult to learn anything at all about the people involved in this itinerant business. Either the system has forgotten about circuses, decided in its organisational monomania that it's too much trouble making up exhaustive rules for such a tiny and eccentric industry, even too much trouble banning it, or the funfair people are intentionally covering up their tracks.

'So, are you with Steaua?' Vasile shouts over the music.

Vasile drives, so gets to choose the music. It's all right listening to Modern Talking, but the man also craves conversation. Now it's football; does Constantin support the army's team?

Constantin searches deep within himself and finds some sympathy for a northern handball club.

Titus pointed out that funfair workers would also be free from the spying eyes of neighbours, a constraint on any other citizen. Behaviour that would raise suspicions in a tower block goes unnoticed in a campervan site.

'The main thing will be to put together a list of the places they've been the last six weeks,' Constantin thinks out loud. 'Should be easier if we have the place names from them and then can just cross-check with the town halls.'

If even only a couple of other locations match the murders, that's as good as case closed. And that's without taking into account any possible testimony by those kids the prostitute mentioned during the interrogation. It could be the same ones he saw the morning of the Old Gorge case. Might he be so lucky? He would recognise them, especially the cartwheel girl. Gap-toothed, brown hair. He can still see her, grinning, just a few paces away from the corpse.

Too many leads are pointing this way for the case not to end with the funfair. Their workers will be athletes, capable of wielding knives, or grappling hooks. Indeed: what degenerate madness, if it turns out more than one person was in on the killing spree. Instinctively, Constantin's hand goes to his service weapon.

Davidescu actually called ahead at the police station in Copşa Mică and requested that four of their policemen accompany Constantin and Vasile into the funfair. But Constantin refused their help. He wants to observe the funfair workers' reactions to his questions. If the police barge in on them in great force, there will be no room for nuance.

'I saw you're driving a Trabant,' Vasile suddenly says. 'You've tried applying for another car? What would you go for?'

Constantin sighs. What can he talk about with this man? There are only three types of cars in the entire country, and they still have four hours of death-haunted land to cross.

'Fuck me,' Vasile says as they drive into the town.

They have been driving northwards forever only to arrive at something of an underworld, a coalmining town with soot-blackened houses, bare trees with thin black branches, and an afternoon skyline of industrial chimneys that spew ashen smoke. Constantin can't help gaping through the smudgy windscreen. Even the people are covered in the stuff; everyone looks like a chimney sweep. Vasile pulls up the collar of his shirt.

'What a place,' Constantin says.

Like Vasile, he has a sudden urge to cover up his mouth and nose, to wash his hands. He tries to remember if he's ever seen a newsreel of Ceauşescu visiting this place. How would they have stage-managed that, how would they have cleaned up a main road enough, sucked the black clouds out of the sky, to make it look like socialist utopia on TV? But of course he doesn't remember – his brain shuts down the second the Dear Leader's face appears on the screen. In fact, he's pretty sure twenty million brains shut down at that exact moment.

A shepherd and about a dozen sheep are coming slowly down the side of the road; human and sheep both look like they have rolled in soot. Only the shepherd's eye-whites are glistening, and when the man turns his face to them it's as if the whole town is staring.

'Check your weapon,' Constantin says. 'We won't split up. At some point it might make sense to retreat without making an arrest even if we think we've found our man.'

Vasile nods nervously.

They find the funfair in the middle of packing up again. Trailers are being filled and enormous lengths of tarpaulin rolled up. Constantin spins on his heels, sizing up the men of the fair; he notices three young lads and a wiry middle-aged man who would be physically capable of the job. Then he remembers to look for the urchins. He bends to look under carts, knocks on trailer doors. People are mostly not minding them.

The place has an air of haphazard industriousness. Vasile has to assert some police authority to get anyone at all to stop what they're doing and talk to them.

But it all changes when these people hear they are investigating the murders. They are not aggressive, no. Two women exchange glances then nod ruefully. Everyone around Constantin and Vasile suddenly looks dejected. A muscly, beret-and-moustachioed fellow lets fall the front end of a trailer he had been trying to hook to a truck. He sighs deeply and says, 'I'll fetch 'em.'

Two men show up, and they all go to the police car together, out of earshot of the rest of the funfair, who have dropped what they were doing and appear suspended in grim expectation. Everyone looks almost cartoonishly guilty. Constantin cannot quite believe what he's seeing. Vasile has noticed it too, and the expression on his face is as though the murderer is already caught and sentenced.

It has just stopped raining, and the site is little more than a barren field. Constantin is ankle-deep in mud, there's water in his left shoe. One of the men, who says he's the funfair manager, hops on the hood of the police car and offers them a local cigarette, and when Constantin refuses he says, 'Can't blame you, it's a dried-spinach excuse for tobacco. But what else do we have?' He seems perfectly at ease. Constantin is puzzled. People are terrified of the police even when they're not being investigated for multiple murders.

The second fellow, at least, looks suitably miserable.

'On March the sixteenth,' Constantin starts, 'the funfair was in the vicinity of the roadside picnic area where there was a murder.'

The funfair manager nods. 'But Fram was already on his merry way by then.'

'Fram?'

'Fram the Kissy Bear is what we called him,' the manager says, puffing on his cigarette. 'When he raised his head to sniff the air,' the man says, raising his head to illustrate his words, 'he was doing a funny thing with his lips, set them fluttering, you know, like the hem of a frilly dress? Up and down in a ripple; looked as if he was tasting the air with them. Or, yeah – just dying for a kiss.' He shakes his head. 'Sounds cute but believe me it was fucking terrifying.'

'Hold on a sec,' Constantin says. Damn Davidescu, damn the official lies. Of course these people expect he's after their bear. He is trying to think how to rephrase his enquiry when Vasile says, 'So where's the animal?'

105

'Well, here's the thing,' the manager says, and somehow there seems to be no way around it, they are talking about these people's bear. Constantin bites his tongue; he will ask his questions after this charade.

They learn that the second man is the bear handler, and that he had slowly grown frightened of his own bear; was plying the animal with cheap booze instead of actually trying to train him. The man appears to shrink before their sight as the story is told. 'He was going mad on me,' he interrupts, his eyes wide. He bangs a fist on the hood of the police car.

Vasile is furiously taking notes. 'Could he have been bitten by something, got rabies?' he says.

The bear handler shakes his head. 'No, no. I mean mad like us, like folk. Losing it.'

There's alcohol on the man's breath. He's probably one of those permanent drunkards.

'How exactly did the animal escape?' Vasile asks.

'I couldn't sleep any more,' the bear handler interrupts, 'I had nightmares. Horrible, horrible nightmares!'

'We were on the road, in between gigs,' the manager says. 'Bogdan just found the cage open in the morning.'

'Is that so?' Vasile says.

The manager shrugs, points his cigarette at a nearby slat fence covered with peeling posters. 'Fram is on all our posters, he was our star – if you think punters appreciate seeing Bogdan in a fur coat instead of the bear they were promised, you're welcome to the show.'

'How well trained is the animal?' Vasile asks. 'Are there special command words, or does he only listen to Bogdan?'

'He does all the tricks a bear can do with half a bottle of vodka in his system,' the circus manager says. 'None at all without.'

'He stands on his hind legs and waves,' Bogdan says. 'Sometimes he'll spin around.'

'But isn't he trained?' Vasile insists.

'Told you already – it's his liver that's trained.'

'Where have you been the last two months?' Constantin interrupts.

'The last two months, crikey . . .' The manager takes a moment to think and then he lists eight towns. Constantin writes it all down; some places must be tiny because he's never heard of them. He will need a map to compare it with the locations of the murders. 'You report to the local authorities in every new place, correct? I expect the authorities to corroborate this list.'

The manager nods. 'But I just told you, we haven't seen our bear in more than three months.'

Vasile nods along with them like an idiot.

'Are there any kids around?' Constantin asks.

'It's a funfair,' the manager says.

'I mean, your children. Do you have children travelling with the funfair?'

The manager now looks offended. 'I thought at least the police are above believing the slander that us gypsies steal children.'

Constantin raises a hand. What a cursed thicket of misunderstandings. He explains he is looking for witnesses.

'But the man just told us the bear was gone by then,' Vasile says, and Constantin has never come closer to using his service gun.

They tell Constantin there's a babe in arms and two toddlers, and the rest of them are teenagers, already helping out with the funfair work. They have IDs for everyone, the manager says. Constantin's heart sinks.

Vasile insists they make a note of where the funfair got the bear from eight years ago, the exact location of where it escaped, the bear's ear tag. By way of goodbye, the manager says he understands it looks fishy, but he can't imagine it's their Fram who's done all the killings; that bear is 'lazier than a dead man's eye'. He adds that they wouldn't mind getting him back if the police do catch him.

The manager really does seem innocent. Constantin is beginning to think that if there's a case here it's that they should be arresting the handler for negligence – he's sure the fellow was so overwhelmed by fear that he let the bear run free.

Constantin then asks to speak with the funfair's 'strongman', the moustache-and-beret fellow he noticed earlier.

The man is Hungarian and the funfair manager has to translate some words. He stands awkwardly in front of them, a broad-shouldered, big man who looks like he never stopped feeling small. Constantin has no experience of being face to face with a serial killer, but he would reasonably expect some cunning, repressed rage, confidence or shiftiness . . . The man before him is like a large child. Constantin takes his prints, and the funfair manager's, but even as he's doing it he would bet his green ink pens that he will never come across these prints again.

'The dates fit, the bear's been gone all this time,' Vasile says when they are back in the car. He steals a glance at Constantin, who's busy taking off shoes and wet socks ahead of the long trip home. 'You don't think it's this one because he's not properly trained?'

'The bear stepped out of your damn mouth, man,' Constantin says. 'It's your bear.'

When he comes home that evening, much later than usual, Sandu comes running to the door, gives him a big hug. The boy waits until he takes his shoes and coat off and then he grabs Constantin's hand. They go into the kitchen.

The table is only set for two – he had told Tina he would be late – but looks untouched. The small enamelled pot is on the stove. Constantin lifts the lid: courgette stew. It's cold.

'We didn't eat, Daddy,' Sandu says.

Constantin goes into the living room, finds it empty, then to the bedroom. Tina isn't there either, but some clothes of Alina's are strewn on the bed. Constantin steadies himself for the wave of sorrow that suddenly buffets the room. The girl's favourite doll has also been taken out of its keepsake box and rests face down on the bed.

He finds Sandu sitting on the floor in the little hallway outside the closed bathroom door. Constantin sits down on the other side.

'Shall we play something?'

'Yes!' Sandu jumps up, runs to the kitchen and returns with a deck of cards. 'Seveners!' he says, the way he always does instead of 'sevens', and hands the deck to Constantin for shuffling.

He lays out the cards on the carpet.

Sandu is excited.

They are halfway through the first game when Constantin says, 'I've never seen anyone as tired as your mother was the first six months after you were born.' He doesn't need to raise his voice; the bathroom door is wafer thin. 'Your sister was still a toddler, your mother was working, and you, little man, seemed to want to cry all night.'

He hears a shuffling noise in the bathroom.

'There must have been whole weeks when she didn't get more than one or two hours of sleep at night. I was trying to help, but you know how it is – sometimes a baby only wants its mother.'

Sandu isn't really listening; his focus is on the cards in his hands.

'But the thing is . . . I never saw your mother wake up and feed you or try to calm you with anything other than love in her eyes. I mean . . . you were a tyrannical little shrimp back then, but she already loved that little shrimp to the point of completely forgetting her own suffering.'

Sandu lays down a nice sequence of five court cards.

'We can only imagine how much she loves you now,' he says.

They are on the second game when the bathroom-door handle moves and Tina comes out. She has her back to them. She steps carefully around Sandu's feet and goes to the kitchen. Turns on the stove, adds a third plate.

They sit down to eat.

*   *   *

Back in the office the following day, Constantin is looking out of the window thinking of Tina. For some time now he has been meaning to buy her something nice. A dress? Something soft and colourful. Something to tempt her out of the darkness.

He could try to run to the shops during his lunch break, he thinks, when he hears Maria the secretary's voice. The way she calls his name, he already knows what has happened: another fax has arrived, another death. Another set of gruesome photos.

Constantin feels like throwing up every time. He stands up and slowly walks to her desk.

He's looking at a woman's mutilated body, found in the basement of a shoemaker's shop. He checks the location: hundreds of miles from where they met the funfair people. The killer is definitely not waiting for the police to catch up.

Constantin watches the fax come to a halt then returns to his desk. He studies the grainy photos with a magnifying glass. The phrase *the animal has been destroyed* comes to him: it's what they say when they've put down an aggressive pet, or an irredeemably injured horse. It suggests a violent but careless process, completely impersonal. The phrase carries none of the emotions usually associated with murder, and is therefore less than what a human, even a human who's a target for violence, is worth.

That's what these bodies look like: *the animal has been destroyed*.

How is it possible that murders that appear to be committed in a fit of rage are so clean, evidence-wise? Most of the toxicology reports came back with nothing; a few recorded moderate alcohol intake, but nothing more. Sexual violence is ruled out. There are no fingerprints or any other pieces of physical evidence. The victims are always alone at the critical moment, even when they are in a place where there's no reason to be confident that they would be alone. It's as though the murderer materialises at exactly the optimal moment for the crime.

'You know what I was thinking? A drunk bear can do that just as well as a sober one,' Vasile says, tapping the pile of photos. The previous day in the car, the constable had in full earnestness claimed that he had merely guessed the true culprit, rather than invented him.

'Do I look like goddamn Nostradamus?' Davidescu shouts at the phone after he has hung up.

One thing that Davidescu was right about was that making the killings public has brought a lot more attention on the police, and a lot more pressure. *What are you doing about it? Has there been any progress?* The phones are ringing non-stop: Party people, relatives of Party people, journalists, concerned citizens from within a hundred miles of wherever the last attack took place. There is a switchboard that in theory should shield them, but their direct phone numbers have become black market currency. Neighbours have knocked on Constantin's door at home and timidly asked for updates; he knows all the underground bear rumours.

Davidescu is a bundle of nerves. He's worn a rut in the middle of the office and looks permanently on the verge of punching someone.

Constantin is only halfway through the new file when a

thought comes to him. He digs up the calendar with the dates of the murders circled in red.

'I'm an idiot,' he mutters. 'A fucking idiot.'

He takes the calendar and runs out of the office, doesn't stop until he's at the university. He finds Titus behind his desk. The man puts his finger to his lips when Constantin bursts in and then presses the 'play' button on the cassette player.

For a second, Constantin is happy that he's not hearing the opening notes of that insane troll march. Then he recognises this new tune: the circus theme.

'Ah, for the love of God,' Constantin says. 'Shut up and listen to this.'

He puts the calendar on Titus's desk.

'What do you see?'

Titus looks at the circled dates. He shrugs. 'If it's not a corpse, I don't know what to do with it.'

'Come on! The weekends! Three of the murders happened on consecutive weekends, well out of the nearest towns. Towns that are several hundreds of kilometres apart. Places that are difficult to reach without a car.'

It takes Titus a moment to remember that one of the national saving measures is that car usage has to alternate at weekends depending on whether your registration number is even or odd. Finally, his face lights up. 'Aha! Yes. Hang on – who exactly is exempt from the weekend rule?'

'I've got to ask. It's a particular licence plate format. But for sure it's institutional vehicles, high-ranking civil servants, military and Securitate officers, foreign students . . .'

'I know a hotel manager who brags about being able to drive whenever,' Titus says.

'Yeah,' Constantin says. 'I think anyone in a job where they can do really nice favours can get one.'

'Funny nobody offered it to me,' Titus says.

It will be more than ten thousand people, Constantin thinks. That's not a suspect list. Still, once they have a suspect they'll know to look for an exempt licence plate.

'Let's think,' Constantin says. 'Could there be another explanation? Is it possible that someone has access to two cars with odd and even registration numbers? Hitchhiker?'

'Hang on,' Titus says, 'what happened at the funfair?'

Constantin just waves a hand. 'Their statements check, they weren't anywhere near the other crimes. Look, let's focus on what we have. And there's something else that's strange . . .'

He explains to Titus how it's a miracle of the very worst kind that no one so far seems to have heard or seen anything of use. 'One woman was living with five other persons – and still, he caught her home alone.'

Titus looks sceptical. 'You are saying . . .'

'I'm saying it's someone who somehow knows all these seemingly random people across the country, and knows what they do with their time.'

'Well. For instance, a Securitate agent can travel freely and has the necessary info about the victims from informers' reports.'

Constantin raises his arms in the air, 'True. But also, no. I already requested any files the Securitate had on the victims, I thought they might come in handy.'

'And?'

Constantin kicks the desk. 'No. That's the infuriating thing. It's not the kind of information that's there. They only write things that are seditious, or potentially seditious. Or compromising.'

'Have you asked for any original reports on them? Maybe they're this detailed and they've just been edited.'

Constantin shakes his head. 'It's not there. *Citizen Mihai Dobrin goes fishing every Sunday morning at five a.m.* is not there.'

Titus puckers his lips. 'So . . . how would anyone know?'

Constantin is tired of his own voice, of his thoughts going in circles. 'It's just impossible that one man has a personal connection to these wildly different people in twelve different parts of the country. Yet it seems as if whoever did it has intimate knowledge of their habits. It doesn't add up.'

Titus taps a folder that's on his desk. He leans back in his chair. 'I am looking at these injuries and thinking, hell, maybe it is a bear. I mean, if you hadn't told me what happened . . .'

'Don't you start, too.'

After work he goes wandering in the half-empty department store. He is exhausted from reading the new case file and poring over the photos, but today is as good a day as any to get Tina her present. He still doesn't know exactly what to buy. He drifts from floor to floor. Colour is in short supply, as is softness. The sales attendants eye him suspiciously; one shouts at him from near the window where she's having a smoke, 'This floor doesn't exist, you'll have to go down or up.'

But it's just dreary housecoats everywhere, and plasticky

formal-looking blouses. He wonders if it's intentional, if everything is meant to be reminiscent of uniforms and offices. On the top floor he finds a glass counter with some bits of inexpensive jewellery, and his eyes fall on a bracelet, just a string of small turquoise stones. He feels better walking out of the grey store with the bright stones in his pocket.

In the evening the three of them sit down for the news; Constantin with one eye on Sandu. About a year ago, the boy went through a phase when he would angrily shout 'The rat! The bad rat!' as soon as Ceaușescu's face appeared on the screen, and Constantin is still anxious for the first few minutes of patriotic chants and poems. There was nothing political about Sandu's disgust, nothing the boy had heard from him or Tina: out of all the faces in the world, he just couldn't stand this one. It was almost like an allergic reaction. They had tried everything, down to showing him pictures of actual rodents, pointing out differences, but he only stopped once they threatened him: no playtime, no fairy tales, no cocoa in the morning.

It had been almost funny, in an awful way. Constantin remembers feeling pride that his four-year-old son could see through the televised chants and the fake smiles and recognise this thug of thugs, this erstwhile cold-blooded enforcer, for the filthy rat that he is.

Tonight, the televised Ceaușescu-worship passes without a reaction from Sandu. But Constantin himself is in for punishment as the news will announce the twelfth killing. He makes himself sit through the whole thing: the newsreader's mournful face, the map with the crosses, the reassurances about the army's involvement.

'We will get used to this, too,' Tina says, her face impassive. She says it to the TV, like she's stating a fact. The turquoise bracelet is on the kitchen table, the box unopened.

They watch the zoo bear circle his cage. Constantin closes his eyes and thinks of outer space.

Sandu pokes him in the side. 'Daddy will catch the bad bear.'

Will he, though? He has memorised the details of the cases, he can hold them up before his mind's eye like a deck of cards. Twelve court cards – the victims. The locations scattered across the country in no obvious pattern. By all accounts, the victims did not know each other. The varying ages and sex of the victims rules out a sexual motive. The modus operandi, on the other hand, has been fairly consistent: the victims were all slashed with a hook-like weapon. The bodies are never moved from the scene of the attack. And there are no credible witnesses, not a single one: the few people who have come forward claiming they witnessed an attack had a history of mental illness, and their claims were as outlandish as they were unverifiable; all jokers.

'Fairy-tale time!' Sandu jumps off the sofa.

Constantin picks up Sandu and the green ink book, and they go to the bedroom. They snuggle down in the fairy-tale armchair.

'Here we go,' Constantin says. 'Once upon time there was a tall and gangly devil, with a narrow face that looked as though his head had been squeezed in a doorway. That's unlucky enough, but this devil of ours also happened to belong to one of the lower orders of devilhood. Without much in the way of powers, he had to rely on his wit.

'Ah, but he was a hardworking fellow. Every morning he set out into the village and planted a little seed of worry in people's minds. He went to the market and said to a man who had just bought a sow, "Dear neighbour, it breaks my heart to see how one man will take advantage of another," telling him the animal had swine fever and he'd been cheated. Later, he'd stop by another man's house and ask if he'd fallen out with his wife, because he'd just seen her with another fellow, or he'd help a woman carry water from the well, and on their way home he'd say that a neighbour was casting evil spells on her child.

'In the evenings, the devil went home and lit the fire in the hearth. In that fire he saw everything that went on in the village: how husbands and wives argued with each other and how previously good neighbours hurled curses across fences. Our devil spent the whole night chuckling and writhing with pleasure at the suffering he had caused, while the villagers, burning with suspicion and hatred, tore their hair out.

'One day, a poor wandering idiot came to the village, with only a goat, a straw hat and a knapsack to his name. An old man stopped the fool and his goat for a friendly chat. Was he staying or just passing through, had he come for the market? The pear tree in front of my house is a good place to leave the goat, the old man advised; the animal would have shade and fallen fruit to eat.

'Our devil happened to hear this. As soon as the fool was alone again, the devil went to him, a concerned look on his face. "That old man, he's just after that goat of yours, you see," the devil said. "When night falls he'll untie the goat and lead it away. He's done it before."

118

'In the evening the devil went home, pleased with his day's work. He lit the fire and looked into it, and what do you think he saw? The fool giving the goat to the very old man he had been warned against. "You should have just said so, sir, that you want this poor goat! Every day I worry about not being able to feed her." In return, the old man welcomed the fool as a guest in his house.

'Very well, the devil thought, I can work with this. The next morning he waited until the fool set out about the village, and then he knocked on the old man's door. *Didn't he know the fool was a famous miscreant, wanted in twelve counties for worming his way into people's homes and robbing them of all they were worth? Who but a villain would do such a crazy thing as to give away his goat?* When the fool returned from his wanderings he found his knapsack in the middle of the road.

'That night, the devil watched the old man. Unable to close his eyes in bed, the old man brought the goat into the house. Countless times he shuffled to the door and windows to make sure they were shut. By morning he had burned down three candles. The fool, meanwhile, had climbed a tree and curled up in a hollow.

'The next day, our devil was out and about in the village when the fool grabbed his sleeve. "I don't know how to thank you, sir, for helping me find a good home for that goat. I'm so lucky in my little burrow: it's dry and warm, and it doesn't cost me a farthing, but there's hardly room for me and my shadow in there. Where would I have put the poor goat? We'd both still be homeless if it weren't for you!"'

Constantin pauses: when he thinks of himself as a child, or

a young man, he's sure he had a decent aptitude for happiness. If his memory is accurate.

'What did the devil do then, Daddy?' Sandu asks.

'Oh, the mean devil tried his tricks several times after that, but the fool was just too foolish and innocent for any suspicion to take root in his heart. Worse, the other villagers slowly came to appreciate the fool's ways. They saw how he was always cheerful and innocent, clear as the sky, and they began to care a little less about all the poison the devil was pouring into their ears. There were nights the devil didn't have a single fight to watch. Everywhere he saw only peacefully sleeping folk, and he still writhed, but now it was in agony. His body twisted, and little by little his head started turning the wrong way around. And if he hasn't died then he's still roaming that village muttering to himself, just an angry old devil with his head turned the wrong way.'

Constantin mimes the shape of the devil's head and Sandu giggles. They chat a little longer, and then the boy finally accepts it's bedtime. Afterwards Constantin grabs a light jacket and tiptoes out of the flat.

He has taken to walking alone at night. There were never many people out after dark anyway – everything is closed except for the worst kind of boozers, and street lighting has been non-existent for years – but since the killings there's truly not a soul in the streets. Just the odd car passing by.

He hopes the solitude and quiet will help clear his head. It's as though he has forgotten something, or missed something, a vital clue that will unlock the whole case. A string of killings should be a messy affair, full of mistakes and an ever-growing pile of leads. It's not repetitive and perfect. It's not clockwork.

If he were to be attacked, Constantin thinks, staring ahead down the dark street, he'd better find the strength to leave some clue that even poor Vasile will understand.

Constantin walks for two hours and the next morning at the station he realises Davidescu must have driven past him at night, probably returning from one of his lady friends, because the police chief is looking at him with even less sympathy than usual. In fact, with actual suspicion.

'Out all night,' Davidescu muses ominously, 'yet he wouldn't spot a fanny if it had neon lights.' He points Constantin out to the other men in the office, 'I'll never forgive myself if it turns out fucking Bambi here is our killer.'

Constantin decides not to pay any attention to him. He goes to his desk.

'Don't bother sitting down, you're going on a trip.' Davidescu throws a fax on his desk. 'Another murder popped up. An older one. They think this dead shopkeeper could be the bastard's first victim.'

7

Sighişoara and Piteşti, June

Lia is in the bathroom at home, making faces at herself in the mirror. She sticks her tongue out, makes her eyebrows go as high up on her forehead as possible. Then she tests a more normal face, like the one she uses for answering Comrade Sava's questions in class. Then a sleepy face. Then she tilts her head back and glances down at her nose, the way a musketeer might look at a despised enemy.

'You've been in there forever!' Mother shouts from the kitchen.

It doesn't show, Lia thinks. It's hard to believe, but the biggest secret she's ever had, one of the biggest secrets anyone has ever had, she's sure, does not show on her face.

Constantin has a good memory for places, and easily finds his way to the old town. He parks the car below the citadel and closes his eyes. Of all the places in the world where the bear could have started his killing spree . . . Constantin has been here before, some ten years ago, with Tina. Their first holiday together, in his uncle's Wartburg 353, a tin box of a car with an engine so loud they had to shout at each other throughout the drive. At the time, Constantin and Tina had only been dating for some three months, but things already felt right.

Constantin checks the map then starts on foot towards the police station. He has to walk round the citadel hill. He wonders what kind of reception he'll get. The local cops did well to link their unsolved case to the bear.

It's a pretty medieval town; that's why Tina chose it for a weekend escape. The people here used to have their own ways of building, their own shapes and colours. And despite being much older than most places Constantin is familiar with, this one feels more alive, or more recently alive. Who knows, he thinks, maybe medieval spirits aren't so easily flattened.

He turns a corner and when he looks up the hill he can see the ancient stone wall that goes all the way around, and the side of a defiant fat little tower. The holiday ten years ago comes back to him: waiting in the sun for some figurines in a clock tower to strike noon, walking on cobblestones, drinking sugary lemonades at a wasp-infested garden cafe, running among the Gothic graves in the Saxon cemetery. *Look at all these dead queens!* Tina had exclaimed at the many Reginas on the headstones; Regina must have been a common Saxon name back in the day. They spent a sunny afternoon at a local lido. They had sex in the finally silenced car.

He's glad he didn't bring Vasile: the man's endless, pointless chatter would have felt like an affront to his memories.

Don't lose focus of what you have, Titus had said before Constantin left. Titus had meant the victims; the coroner didn't want Constantin to despair if he ends up returning from this trip, too, without being any closer to a suspect. Titus keeps insisting that the victims can't be random. That, together, they are the key to the case.

He looks at the street, at the people. He's reached the main road and passes empty shop windows. It strikes him how much more sound and colour there is to his memories than to what's in front of him now. He and Tina were loud, they laughed, they listened to foreign music. Tina had bright, summery dresses, patterns and colours that he recognised from afar and which made him want to run towards her like a character in a soppy film. He remembers a soft red leather pouch with creams and perfumes, make-up, women's stuff.

The flattening didn't happen at once.

He snaps right back to the present moment when he walks into the police station. The place even smells the same as the office back home: cigarettes and typewriter ink. He's directed to the first floor, into a windowless office. The local police chief laboriously hands him a tall pile of files he calls 'the Blaga dossier'.

Constantin is most interested in the crime scene and victim photos and what Titus will have to say about them. The rest of the dossier is the profiles of the almost two dozen suspects the local cops had at the start. The investigators insisted on a neighbour the victim had a feud with, and a civil engineer. But there was never any physical evidence incriminating anyone, only apparent motive and opportunity.

'And you say they couldn't have committed the subsequent murders,' Constantin says.

'Correct,' the police chief says. 'Least of all the engineer fellow, who was in jail for two of them. But neither of them have left town since it started.' The chief points at the file. 'There was something there, for sure. The engineer. At first we thought the fellow's wife had been bonking the victim and the jealous husband did him in, but they didn't act like it. I mean, they seem loyal to one another. Tight. Except there's something they're not telling, I'm sure. Even the kid in that family is weird. The last idea we had was that the dead guy had done something to the girl.'

Constantin winces. He has managed to avoid being assigned cases that involve children. It's one thing to detach yourself and trust the legal process when dealing with people who have hurt other adults, and an entirely different thing . . .

'I know,' the man says, though Constantin hasn't spoken. 'Ugly business.'

Ugly or not, if this was the bear's doing and the father has an alibi for the other murders, then it's irrelevant to the case. Unless, of course, the investigators stumbled upon the common denominator between all these seemingly random killings. Child abuse, of some kind.

Constantin closes his eyes.

'Bottom line – you're taking this off our hands, yes?' the police chief speaks again. 'I mean, you have the whole file. I told you everything I know. We agree that this must be the bear's first victim. We're done here, yes?'

Constantin nods and stands up; makes to leave.

'Do you mind if I get that in writing?' The man pushes a piece of paper in front of Constantin. A pen.

'Is this really necessary?'

The police chief gives him a look. 'I want all traces of bear paws off my desk.'

Back out in the street with the absurdly voluminous dossier in his arms, Constantin decides to go straight to the post office and fax the photos to Titus; the coroner is the final authority on whether they are looking at another bear murder. The police station's fax was out of order. Crossing the main road, he has a view of the citadel in the distance, and another past detail comes to him: he and Tina spoke about moving here eventually. They spoke about how happy a child would be in a place like this. A citadel. A clock tower. Endless forests around.

The files are getting heavy and he picks up pace. He averts his glance from the black bear-warning posters that are plastered on a public signboard. There's always a jolt of shame, not just at having failed to put an end to the killings, but at being complicit in this 'a bear did it' nonsense. Davidescu would have a good laugh at his discomfort. *Detective, who exactly insisted on warning the public?*

They might have really moved to this town, but by the time Constantin started working, people no longer just moved somewhere, not any more; they went where they were sent. *The country has needs*, they told him. There's an empty office somewhere you have no family, no friends, no roots, that perversely is yours. Constantin still remembers, two years or so after the holiday, opening the letter with his official allocation.

He had hoped until the last moment. What kind of magic is at work, to make people so pliable? How does anyone placidly come to accept that it's a lottery, the place where they'll live their whole life? He shakes his head to himself on the street, attracts glances from passers-by.

He forces his thoughts back to the case.

What if the killer was also here on holiday? Some kind of tour guide? Now, that would be something. He quickly runs through the other murder locations in his head, but no, there's no such pattern. Who wants to holiday near an oil field?

An oil field. That smell.

The Wartburg ten years ago had been uncomfortable to sleep in, hard and unyielding, and they didn't have money for a hotel. It was summer, and still warm after nightfall, but Tina baulked at just sleeping in a field under the stars. She had an idea: they could sneak up on the roof of a tower block. They'd still see the stars, but at least there wouldn't be any bugs or animals.

He finally reaches the post building, and goes straight behind a counter, offloads the files on a desk. The employee having her breakfast sizes him up; he shows her his badge. Explains. Their fax machine is in a back office, she says. She has to check with the director. He can wait over there.

One of the men waiting at the counter for the woman to finish her sandwich looks at Constantin and mumbles, 'Great, another clever one.'

He and Tina had a full day around town, and left it very late, too late to reasonably pretend that they were paying a visit to some relative or friend. The blocks they went into, giggling, tipsy, they were immediately challenged by the residents.

Old men, walking stick pointed menacingly, or housewives returning from the bins: who exactly were they looking for? What kind of visiting hour is this? In most blocks they didn't make it past the ground floor. Repeatedly and frustratingly found out, they rebelled. They pretended to be offended by the interrogations, or they offered absurd names. Surely the Comrade must know his own neighbour Agamemnon? Yes, Agamemnon, who has the pretzel shop downtown? They would flee laughing, only stopping several streets away to catch their breath. It was fun, but Constantin eventually said they must pull themselves together or they'd be spending another night squashed in the Wartburg. *There's a right way to do this.* They've got to read the names on the postboxes, choose a top-floor resident, and have a reasonable excuse for why they're so damn late. When they meet someone on the landing, they must speak first, not wait for the inevitable questioning. They looked respectable enough if they could only stop giggling like kids.

It worked, and after two blocks in which they managed to get all the way to the top only to find the roof hatch padlocked, they finally got lucky. Up the ladder, through the hatch, and they were back under the stars.

The post office employee has reappeared; she shouts, 'Comrade Police!' over the counter. He picks up the stack again. He feels the queuers' resentful glances on his back.

'I'm operating it,' the woman says once they're in a back office. 'It's on me if you break it.' Her eyes widen when she opens the folder with the photos. 'It's true, then?' she whispers. 'The beast was here.'

Constantin has the authority to ask this woman to leave, but not the energy. He lets her slowly feed the photos into the fax. She is fascinated by each image. 'That must have hurt,' she says at a photo of a slash in the man's side, a tiny severed tube-like organ visible inside the cut.

The rooftop smelled strange, but it didn't matter. They were tired. There was a breeze. Constantin spread out their beach blanket, and they used his backpack for a pillow. They undressed. They didn't even bother to think what the strange smell was, not until they woke up at dawn with an utterly sinister headache, and an enginey, dirty taste in their mouths. Their skin felt sticky, and as their eyes got used to the weak light they realised what that smell was: pitch tar. The roof must have just been insulated with the stuff. Flakes of it had got everywhere, tiny hellish black flakes; it stuck to their hair and to their clothes. Constantin first peeled the blanket off the roof, then abandoned it there in disgust. They climbed down and drank all the water they had on the landing of the block, but they still felt poisoned. Tina started crying. She had a fear of throwing up, still has it. They went and tried to wash it off in the river, but the stuff was like glue. Constantin remembers lying on his back in the grass and wishing there was some way to scrub himself clean on the inside. And on the way back home, he actually said it: that once he had a job he would have money for a hotel, and anyway, *they will send us on annual holiday*. He said it like he looked forward to it. Being sent on holiday, the government choosing the spot.

'You know what the good thing is?' the post office woman

suddenly says. She waves a photo at him. 'At least the beast is done with our town.'

'I want to make it clear from the start that we don't think you had anything to do with Comrade Blaga's death,' Constantin is saying. After faxing the photos he decided to get his car and pay the engineer suspect a visit. The police chief said the family was hiding something, and if the victim was some kind of abuser it could be relevant to the case.

He's in the Stoians' living room, addressing the couple, and trying to avoid staring at the contraption hanging from their ceiling light – an elaborate garland made of paper strips and empty Easter-egg shells; red, blue, green and yellow. Here and there on the walls are colourful children's drawings and torn pages from what looks like old magazines, probably advertisements – a photo of a seascape and a ship, a tiger-patterned bedsheet. When he walked in he noticed that an inside door handle is covered in what he hopes is red nail varnish. An inflated orange water wing sits atop the TV.

It's the first time he can remember being genuinely surprised by someone's home. He understands why this family stands out in the eyes of the local police: there's nothing illegal here, yet this home screams disobedience. He's also aware that his first reaction, his gut reaction, was resentment. *How dare they? Who do they think they are?* It takes conscious effort from him to switch to *how lovely to see something different.* A switch that leaves him a bit dazed, as though he's just done a somersault.

'We've done everything we can to help,' the woman says. 'But we hardly knew the man.'

Constantin is listening for any sounds from the other rooms. He hasn't asked to speak to the child.

'You were seen entering his apartment,' he says. 'Just a few days before he died.'

'I've told them a million times,' the woman says. 'There was a rumour Blaga was looking for a shop apprentice. My cousin's son wanted to postpone his military service; his father had fallen very ill and the boy wanted to stay here and help.'

Suddenly there's a whining noise from beyond a door, and next a proper howl. The door bursts open and a small child runs in, makes straight for his mother. 'He ate my foot! He ate my foot!' he cries. The woman picks him up and cradles him in her arms. Huge tears stream down his face. He has pillow marks on a cheek.

The boy keeps pointing at his feet.

'Silvia, we've got to stop letting him watch the news,' the boy's father says.

'I didn't think he understood,' the woman whispers.

The boy is a couple of years younger than Sandu, Constantin thinks. Too young to have authored the drawings.

They wait for the boy to stop crying, and then the woman sits back down with them.

'It's odd you went to the home of a man you didn't know well,' Constantin goes on, 'rather than discuss the opportunity with him in the shop.'

The woman shakes her head. 'Yes, it was stupid,' her husband speaks before she has a chance. 'But the fact remains we had nothing to do with his death. You know they locked me up and questioned me for two weeks?'

The woman takes her husband's hand in hers and gives it a supportive squeeze. The police chief was right, they are not enemies. Constantin is ambushed by a pang of jealousy. The most painful memory is not of himself and Tina happy in this town, but what they believed then their future would be like.

'You're not suspects, not any more.' Constantin looks the man in the eyes, tries to get through to him. 'I'm here because the authorities are considering that maybe this is not the perpetrator's only murder. We are trying to understand as much as possible about the victims, to see if they are not as random as it superficially seems.'

'But weren't the police thinking it's the bear?' the man says.

'Not necessarily,' Constantin says. Damn Vasile and his stupid idea. Once again, he can't even ask the normal questions an investigator would ask – how can he claim that a bear's attacks are anything other than random? 'If you have any information about the deceased that the authorities are ignorant of, it would help if you'd tell us.'

The two appear reticent. It's obvious they're still very afraid.

'Whatever you tell me will not be used against you. You have my word.'

'Why would we know something the authorities don't?' the man asks. He laughs to himself at the absurdity of the suggestion.

'Did he, for instance, hurt you in any way? Did he hurt your daughter?'

Constantin then points at the walls, wants to say that this looks like the work of parents trying to compensate the child for something, but he bites his tongue. He might be wrong, or they might misunderstand. He doesn't want to be the reason the drawings are taken down.

'Our daughter went to his shop to buy something,' the woman says. 'Blaga realised that she was alone and thought it best to bring her home.'

'But the child refuses to answer any questions about that day.'

'I gave her a bad spanking – the girl took money from Silvia's purse without asking. She just wants to forget everything about that day.'

He gives them his number and tells them to call him in case they remember anything. 'Confidentially,' he adds, although it's a lie because any call might be listened to. He tries not to judge them. The crucial thought that they could help has simply not entered their minds, and Constantin cannot put it there. And they're right, sort of; altruism is a lot to ask for, in this time and place.

On his way out, Constantin tries to get a good look at the drawings. Clowns, parrots, Indians, castles, cartoon figures, dwarfs. There doesn't seem to be anything sinister in any of them.

It's after seven o'clock and it's suddenly quiet. Lia is alone at the bench between the two apartment blocks: the kids she had been playing bottle caps with all scattered home when the news started, even the snotty five-year-old who's always trying to get in on their game.

She's thinking about the map of the country that was in the new history textbook the class received today. It was the strangest thing – the map-maker had drawn a bunch of pale flowers into the outline of the country, even made the ribbon of this bunch of flowers unfurl in the place of the Danube. Lia tried to make sense of it, really tried. She squinted at it. She pressed her nose into the page. She closed one eye and blinked quickly with the other until Cauliflower yelled at her, and still that flower-map did not make sense. What the map of the country does look like is a fish, a perfect flatfish. There's a nick in the south-west that is a mouth, and a proper fish-tail at the other end, flapping in the Black Sea. She even showed Ewald the mouth and the tail, but he, instead of thinking about what she'd just said, pointed at a spot that had nothing to do with anything and whispered, 'The bear was there yesterday.'

The bear. Lia remembers now to check for the bear under the bench, then behind her in the vegetable garden. She gets a proper fright when she turns back around. There's a stranger in front of her.

'You're the little artist?' the man asks.

This is not a neighbour. Not a teacher. She doesn't recognise him as the father of a classmate. Lia feels the big secret inside her shrinking into a tiny marble and rolling into hiding.

'I liked your Rumpelstiltskin,' the man goes on.

They're so close to home. She just has to jump off the bench past the stranger and in ten strides she'll be inside the block.

Wait, what?

She steals a glance at the man's face, expects to see the coiled-up bad thoughts behind it, but his eyes are smiling. Lia checks with her belly, waits for it to say something. *Come on.* Her belly has no opinion.

'What do you mean, Rumpelstiltskin?' Lia asks. It can't be wrong to just ask a person what he means. Mother would agree.

The man points at her block. 'I just spotted it on the wall. I was upstairs, speaking to your parents.'

She knows exactly which drawing he means: the evil dwarf, in a green-and-red outfit, who's dancing around a fire. That drawing has place of honour in the living room because it's her favourite. Sometimes, when friends of Mother's come to visit and everybody sits for a coffee, Lia will hang around, will try to avoid being shooed away until the visitors have a chance to look at her drawings. But no one ever says anything. The most she ever gets is an 'Oh!' right when they walk in.

'And I had no idea you could do that with Easter eggs,' the man says. 'I'll have to show my son.'

'You can make it with more eggs,' Lia hears herself speak. 'Mother only gave me six.'

The man smiles. 'So which was the latest drawing?' he says.

Her belly is saying something now, all right; it's shouting it: someone wants to speak to her about her drawings. Her fingers are tingling. She could run up and bring the colouring book.

'The circus tent,' she says. 'Did you see it? It's from when I was training for the competition.'

She tells him about the competition. She hadn't meant to, because the competition somehow sticks together with everything that happened since the bad day, but she tries to use the same words that Mother and Dad use when they talk about it to a neighbour.

The man is really paying attention to her. 'You seem just fine!' he suddenly says. He musses her hair. 'A happy kid. I'm glad.'

Lia doesn't know what to say to this. 'Which one did you like the most?' she asks.

'Told you. Rumpelstiltskin. He has this mischievous look, dancing around the fire.'

Lia rubs her hands together, makes the sneaky face she imagined on the evil dwarf.

'Exactly!' The man laughs again.

He sits down on the bench next to her. Lia is about to ask if he wants to see her colouring book, but his face has changed.

'So you're fine, in general, and you just didn't feel like speaking to the other policemen. Well, I can't really blame you.'

The other policemen. There's a loud noise suddenly in her ears, like a rush of water. *The other policemen.* She wants to give him back all the nice things he just said and run away.

'Hey,' Constantin says, as softly as he can. The kid has turned away from him. 'I'm just trying to make sure—'

'For the love of God!'

An old man has appeared in front of the bench. A neighbour, from the looks of it. He's carrying a canvas shopping bag, and teetering a bit. He's actually scowling at Constantin.

The man is drunk.

'Excuse me?' Constantin says.

'When will you people stop torturing this poor family? She's just a kid!'

Constantin turns back to the girl. 'I'm a policeman, but you've got nothing to worry about. Nor do your parents.' The girl looks so miserable that he can barely stop himself from giving her a hug.

'Don't believe a word he says, kid,' the old man then says.

Constantin laughs in disbelief, except it's really not funny. He looks up at the block windows – anyone could be listening. Is the old man insane? What if it's some kind of test, what if Davidescu set him up so that he must arrest a seditious citizen?

Constantin stands up. The girl is still staring at her shoes. He doesn't want to leave her like this. He could have reassured her if only the old man had minded his own business.

'Endless police visits!' the damn fellow goes on. 'Every other bloody day.'

'A man was killed,' Constantin says. 'What do you suggest the police do, other than investigate?'

'Come on. Everybody knows you people are only putting so much effort into this because he was a snitch.'

An informer? Another informer?

'Don't give me that face,' the old man says. 'Of course we know. Everybody knows!'

Driving back home, Constantin keeps getting ahead of himself, worrying about how the Securitate are bound to obstruct any investigation of their own ranks. But he's not there yet; first he needs proof. Are other victims informers? Could they really all be – and nobody told him, even when he asked for any files the services have on the victims?

Speed and road signs whizz by the car.

He punches the roof of the car, lets out a curse. Most of all he's afraid that he'll get back home, look at the files, and discover, with hindsight, that he could have figured out this detail on his own.

If the victims were all informers it would explain so many things. The wildly different backgrounds, the fact that they're all adults. And it proves his initial gut feeling: there is some additional layer of information that the killer has access to, that enables him to attack his victims at their most vulnerable.

It's beyond belief that it took a random, drunk, stroppy old man to reveal the most important detail of the investigation.

For the millionth time, Constantin goes through the cases in his mind. The third victim was an anaesthetist who had a reputation for demanding bribes to ensure that his patients woke up after operations; another was a head cook at an orphanage, accused of stealing the kids' food supplies. It could well be that these people only dared to pull stunts like these because they felt they had protection. The dead priest: what more reliable stream of intelligence than that provided by a man who runs from the confessional straight to the nearest phone? Another victim, killed while hiking, was a retired professor, and a thing that came up in the investigation was that students hated him for insisting on ideological purity for passing exams. He could easily have been an informer, too.

Constantin wishes Titus were in the car with him. He wishes he had the tape to play the deranged troll opera right now. How should he approach Davidescu with this? The man is a coward. Constantin has to convince a coward to stick his neck out.

*   *   *

'I'm not bringing up a criminal!' Mother shouts, and tries to slap Lia's bottom. Lia manages to run just before Mother reaches her. She locks herself up in the bathroom.

They were all in the kitchen, and Mother and Dad had just asked her what the policeman said, when the phone rang. Mother answered the phone and came back like this.

'Silvia, what on earth?' Dad says.

Lia can hear Mother by the door. 'Are you insane?' Mother keeps yelling. 'To paint a monster over the map of the country!'

What? Mother is angry because of her fish? Lia cannot believe it. She sacrificed half a green crayon to make a nice, bright flatfish with scales, fins and both eyes on one side, just like the picture in Grandpa's atlas. It's not possible that anyone would prefer the stupid bouquet in washed-out colours.

'But it was a fish,' Lia says. 'A nice fish, not a monster, I can show you in my book—'

'Stop lying. Sava told me you painted a creature with many eyes. She said, *I do not know what your daughter was trying to insinuate.* Who gave you permission to insinuate anything, you little brat?'

Lia shakes her head. 'No, that's what the flatfish looks like, it has both eyes on the same side. It's in Grandpa's—'

'Is this family cursed?' Mother cries from beyond the door. 'It's just one thing after another!'

'Will you explain what the hell happened?' Dad says.

'Don't you get it? Sava called to tell us our daughter desecrated the map of the country. She drew a monster over it, a creature with many eyes.'

Dad has gone quiet. Finally he says, 'Silvia, it sounds like a misunderstanding. This kid will draw on anything.'

'No, this is not normal,' Mother says. 'What's the matter with her? Where does she learn to do these things? Who's she been talking to?'

What's *desecrate*? Lia wonders, and why is everybody always mad at her for nothing? She sinks to the floor.

It's like a kind of darkness, the grown-ups' anger, something she can't see through. She hugs her knees to her chest and tries to cheer herself up with thoughts of her big secret. It will change everything. Mother and Dad, Ewald . . . even Cauliflower! They will all thank her one day.

'Let me get this right,' Davidescu says. Constantin caught the police chief just as he arrived at the station, down at the registry desk. He took him by the elbow and pushed him into an empty office.

'You want me to call Securitate and tell them their men are murderers,' Davidescu goes on. 'Why don't we just boil my head now and get it over with?'

'Not like that,' Constantin says. 'What we do is contact each Securitate branch in the towns with a victim and ask them to confirm the dead guy was an informer. Say that it came up in the investigation and may be relevant for narrowing down suspects. Don't tell them any others are informers. Keep it small and local.'

'So what? Step two in your brilliant plan is to boil my head.'

Davidescu has lit a cigarette and is puffing away. An unpleasant thought sneaks up on Constantin: what if he's wrong? What if the rottenness he sees in the case files isn't an actual pattern; what if it's simply the reality that comes up when a totalitarian police force looks at life in a totalitarian state? Everybody is an informer, everybody is corrupt. The notion is so unpleasant he shivers.

'Think about it,' Constantin says. 'If I'm right, it's very likely our murderer has access to high-ranking officials. To classified information. It's a matter of national security. We'll get into trouble if we *don't* warn them.'

Davidescu kicks a paper basket. 'Why didn't the bastards just brief us properly from the beginning?'

Constantin has thought about this. 'They're not aware. I mean, no one is aware that they're all informers. The local stations knew about their individual victim, but they're not used to briefing down, so they neglected to tell the police.'

'And they'll brief us now. Right!' Davidescu says.

'We'll ask them straight out. It's one thing to omit a piece of information, and another to lie, in writing, in a multiple homicide investigation. They won't dare.'

Davidescu stubs out the cigarette on the soil of a wilted pot plant.

'Or I'm wrong and nothing will come of it,' Constantin goes on. 'Please. We could get some answers by the end of today. It's only eight o'clock.'

'I'll tell you what time it only fucking is – it's only 1989. Three years till my retirement.'

But they don't find out anything that day. It takes Davidescu until the afternoon to pen a fax that he feels is safe enough while still asking the actual question. And even then, once he presses 'send', for a few moments the police chief hovers over the fax, looking as though he wants to claw the paper back out of the machine.

Constantin spends the day in a state of fruitless agitation, going through the case files, worrying about how he'll get the police chief to act on the new info once it's confirmed. He takes one of Davidescu's cigarettes and sniffs at it, fiddles with it, until the thing crumbles in his hand. He snaps at Vasile. The end of the day catches him daydreaming about garlanding the police station with confetti and empty Easter eggs.

It doesn't get better once he's at home. Something of that past holiday rubbed off on him, and now it makes him follow Tina around the house. Words hover on the tip of his tongue. He waits in the armchair behind the piano for the last fifteen minutes of her lesson; he watches her heat their dinner; after the news he sits by as she mends a jumper that Sandu snagged on a slide. It's possible that she doesn't even notice him. He wonders how close to her he could get before she would protest.

I feel so sorry for us.

He knows he's being ridiculous, because even when he daydreams himself away, Tina isn't there. This one detail is still implausible, even in his fantasies of long ago or other planets. It's just too far-fetched. What are the words that would suddenly be harmless?

8

Sighișoara, June

Lia is in the classroom, drawing and colouring. She was going to speak to Comrade Sava today, but instead she is drawing. She puts the Earth with its blue seas and green continents in the middle of the page. Then she makes the sun, a yellow fire-bauble, lets it shine on Earth from a safe distance.

Click-clack, the teacher's high heels sound on the floorboards.

It's the third day that she hasn't asked the teacher her question. It's not a nice feeling, not having courage. When she talked to Comrade Mantea about her mission she was excited, but something happened after that. It's like she had the courage then, in front of Comrade Mantea, when she didn't really need it, and none at all now when she has to open her mouth. It feels like empty pockets. Like plunging your hand thinking you'll find that piece of hard candy or chewing gum, when actually Mother sent you to school in the wrong coat.

It's just some words.

145

She makes another bauble, smaller than the others and pink, in the lower right-hand corner. It's purple, really, because there's no pink crayon, but it's meant to be pink. After this she starts on the hero. He's at the top of the page, the bravest explorer of all. She gives him a light blue helmet and matching spacesuit, and he's smiling through his visor. Why the smile? Because he has just realised that the view from outer space is like being deep inside a Christmas tree. And he is never afraid.

Lia smiles back at him. She names the drawing, fattening the black letters across the surface of the sun: *Astronaut.*

Comrade Sava is walking through the rows of school benches; now and again she picks up a classmate's drawing to comment on it.

Lia looks at her spaceman. A little courage, maybe, is that what she feels in her belly? It could go something like this: Comrade Sava loves the space drawing, and when the class is over Lia goes to her desk and opens her mouth and says the words, without her face going funny and Comrade Sava smelling a Mantea-sized rat.

Two more benches and the teacher will be here. Lia takes a deep breath. Cauliflower usually minds about her colours. She once said about a very nice self-portrait: *Child, all you ever really draw is parrots – two-legged parrots, four-wheeled parrots, three-storied parrots.'*

Click-clack. The steps come to a halt. Cauliflower's long fingernail lands on Lia's drawing. The teacher turns the paper upside down. She taps the drawing. Once, twice. 'It's not called astronaut.'

'The spaceman?' Lia says.

146

'We call them cosmonauts,' she says.

Lia is sure that she has come across both words. They both mean spaceman. And anyway it has nothing to do with how good the drawing is. 'Doesn't astronaut mean spaceman?' Lia says.

'The Soviet space traveller is called cosmonaut,' Comrade Sava says.

Lia shrugs. 'This is any space traveller.'

The class giggles.

Bam! The ruler slams down on Lia's desk. 'Call it cosmonaut or spend the rest of the class in the corner!'

The teacher is so angry her chin trembles. And from nothing, Lia thinks, from nothing! But Sava stands over Lia's shoulder, doesn't leave until Lia picks up the eraser. Finally the teacher turns around and continues up the aisle. She puts her hand on the back of Dora's head. 'Let's see your work, dear.'

Lia looks at the drawing again. It can't even be done: erasing the title, as Comrade Sava said, will make a mess of the sun. The teacher can't have meant for her to ruin the whole drawing. Lia drops the eraser and picks up a crayon. The fix is to just draw another spaceman in the left-hand corner of the page. It will work, that bit is too empty anyway. He has to be a bit smaller because there isn't much room left in outer space, but Lia tries to make it up to him by colouring his helmet and suit red. And he, too, is smiling at us. Above him, in somewhat cramped letters, she writes 'Cosmonaut'. There. We now have every type of space traveller.

Lia spins around to see how long before Comrade Cauliflower is back at her desk.

Click-clack. Sava takes a look at the drawing. And then something happens. She snatches the pencil case from Lia's desk and rummages in it until most of the crayons have spilled on the floor. Lia bends over to pick them up, but Sava smacks her over the head.

Lia freezes, like that, half her bottom off her chair.

Clutching the eraser, Sava rubs out the word *Astronaut*. Lia looks on as the sun turns into a smudgy mess. Sava walks away with the ruined drawing and slaps it face down on her desk. Then she comes back, high heels jabbing the floorboards.

'No,' Lia says out loud, without meaning to. At the first smack of the ruler she tries not to cry, at the second not to pee. Sava counts to twenty. Then she drags Lia by the arm down the aisle towards the back of the class. 'Get in the corner!' Sava shouts.

Lia is shaking. Her palms want her to look at them. She doesn't want to look at them, she wants to close her eyes. But if she closes her eyes she will pee for sure. She stares at the wall. She knows this wall. The corner is painted beige, like the rest of the classroom, but there's this one spot the size of a large coin where the paint has worn off. Under the beige paint there's a white layer and underneath it there's another, greenish layer. Under that there's brick. Brick is a nice reddish colour that's the warmest of them all; like a much wiser yellow. The four layers all taste a little differently.

'Look, it's good she's showing interest,' Mother is saying to Comrade Sava. 'There must be some kind of schedule.'

Lia is holding Mother's hand and looking down at her feet,

but inside she's jumping up and down. She has asked Mother about the schedule for the National Day, said that it will be easier for her to prepare if she knows what's going to happen. And Mother agreed.

But Comrade Sava is not replying. Lia is afraid to look up at the teacher's face.

'Where will she have to be, at what time?' Mother goes on. 'What exactly is expected of her?'

'These details are not for you,' the teacher finally speaks. 'There has been official communication from the Party head-quarters to the Town Hall, and the Mayor himself wrote the school a letter with all we need to know. It's taken care of. Your daughter just needs to learn her poems and behave. Lord knows that's challenge enough.'

'A letter?' Lia says.

'You know all you need to know.'

Lia looks around the classroom, at the children settling at their desks. She has the words on the tip of her tongue: *Do you have it here?*

'These details are always kept confidential until the last moment,' Cauliflower says to Mother. 'Surely you must under-stand why that is the case.'

'Well, yes, but we're all in trouble if the child doesn't do well on the day,' Mother says. She sounds like she has given up.

'And whose fault is it we're in this situation?' Sava asks.

There's a meeting going on again in Comrade Mantea's block. Lia lets out a huff and crouches at the foot of the stairs. It doesn't even make sense, the neighbours' nosiness. Why do they care where anyone goes? She couldn't care less what they do. Mother and Dad will sometimes point out a curtain moving in a window. 'See that?' they'll say. 'They're always watching,' and pretend they have just shown her something very important. It's like a stupid game all this watching, except no one ever explained the rules.

'Last night it was just two hundred kilometres from here,' the old administrator is saying. 'Shouldn't we do something?'

It's true. On the news last night, the cross had been the closest ever to their town.

'But what the hell can we do? The thing must weigh at least half a tonne,' another man says. 'And it's all so vague. *Take extra caution around railway stations and bus stops.* What, it's a commuter bear?'

'There might be reasons why the authorities can't reveal all they know,' the administrator speaks again. 'We don't have the full picture, we are not involved in the investigation.'

Unhappy mumblings from up and down the staircase.

'My dad has been refusing to go out since this started,' a woman says in a complaining voice. 'Used to be out all day, out of my hair, playing backgammon in the car park. Now he's in my kitchen with another oldster' – she points at her flat – 'driving me insane with their damn dice rattle.'

'Maybe . . .' an older woman in a beautiful, pink-and-yellow housecoat starts saying something, but stops herself. She looks at the faces of her neighbours. 'Maybe they just don't want us to go out,' she says.

'Mother, let's go in, this is upsetting you.' A younger woman takes her by the elbow and guides her into an apartment.

'I remember a piece of advice about bears, from my hiking days,' says a man who hasn't spoken before. 'Apparently we should be hanging little jingle bells on our backpacks, ding-ding, because bears will avoid humans if they can hear us coming. And that, generally, we should avoid paths frequented by bears. But how do we know a path is frequented by bears, you may ask?' he goes on. 'Well, if there's bear scat on the path. But how does one know that scat is bear scat and not boar or cattle, or deer? Or horse?'

He pauses, waiting to see if anyone knows the answer. People shrug. Lia shakes her head, to encourage the man to reveal his secret.

'You'll know it's bear scat 'cause it's full of jingle bells.'

The whole landing laughs. Lia tries to memorise the joke, step by step, to tell it to Ewald at school.

The neighbours go on like this for a while, and she stops paying attention. She's almost asleep by the time they finish and she can finally knock on Comrade Mantea's door.

'My dear child! I am experiencing great clarity these days,' he says as he shows her into the kitchen. He looks a bit mad, with his grey hair every which way, the threadbare bathrobe and the shiny eyes. He looks very old and very young at the same time. 'Ah, how can I explain it to you?'

'If I don't understand something,' Lia says, 'I take it home with me and I think about it and maybe I understand it later.'

'You are an exceptional child, I hope you know that. Don't ever let anyone tell you anything else. Ah, sometimes I want you to grow up quickly, so that we can talk man to man, you know what I mean, but then I'm terrified that you'll grow up and be just like them!'

'I'll be nine soon,' she says.

He looks disappointed. 'We have to work with what we've got. Look at this!' he says, and points at the table and a plastic box the size of a small book. The box is greyish in colour and covered with a kind of dust. The whole kitchen table is dirty with this dust.

'Do you remember what I said, that everyone is asleep?' he says.

She nods.

'And how do you wake someone?' He bends down to look her in the eye. 'A bang! A great big bang to wake them all up!'

They play a few matchbox games after that, and she tells him the bad news about the letter.

He is not happy. 'We really need those plans,' he says. 'Look, if there's a letter like that teacher of yours says – can't you get your little monkey hands on it? Where would they keep it?'

'In the staffroom? That's where the postman leaves his post.'

She thinks she could take it; the teachers leave the room unlocked when they are teaching. She'll just say she needs the bathroom. Cauliflower will be angry with her but she can say she has a stomach ache.

'Hm, not sure you can just take the letter,' Comrade Mantea says. 'That will make them wonder. Give the game away.'

'The bad people will know,' Lia whispers.

He stops just as he was going to flip the matchstick box.

'Actually, you probably can. The teacher will be too afraid

to admit she lost the damn thing. Ha! We can always count on cowardice.'

Lia can't take it any more at that point and tells him about the troubles with the fish map.

Comrade Mantea listens with his hand covering his mouth. By the end of the story he is looking concerned again.

'Dear child, can't you lay off the devilries for a few weeks?'

'BUT IT WAS A FISH!' she shouts at him.

'Shhh!' he grabs her hand. 'I'm sure you're right, and I'm sure your map is much prettier. But they won't see that, will they?' He grabs hold of her shoulders. 'Do you want to save this country or not?' He looks very serious.

She nods.

'Then you have to try and do what they tell you. Just until the meeting. Otherwise they'll cancel, or send a better child! Do you want to lose this opportunity? All right? Come on, let's play.'

He flips the matchbox high up over the table.

'You know what's getting to me?' he goes on. All of a sudden, he has the face of people who make speeches on the TV. 'Every day I become aware of some new horrible side effect of the way we live. We all complain of having to queue for basic food, the cold in winter, of not being free to speak our minds, but what about culture, what about music and art? That all goes on elsewhere – people collaborate and are inspired by each other's works and build on previous efforts . . . In arts, in science. While we are stuck! Someone pressed the "tread water" button on us. Isn't this yet another form of torture?'

He stares at her.

153

'It's like every day you wake up and discover some new horrible injury on your body.' He looks down at himself.

She nods, even though she doesn't understand. She's afraid that if he notices that she doesn't always understand him he might stop telling her things.

'You know that fairy tale, "The Sleeping Beauty"?' Comrade Mantea asks.

'Yes!'

'Well. What is happening there is that the Princess is sleeping through everything. She's not dead, but she's not alive either. It's a bit like this with all the people around us: they are not dead, they function well enough for eating, sleeping, going to their jobs. Queuing. But an important part of them, the most important part, is dead.'

'Dead,' she says. Grown-ups like it when you repeat what they say.

'Like that cop – harassing a small child for nothing, then pretending not to know that his precious victim was an informer. Bears, goddammit! They invented murderous bears.'

The policeman was strange. Comrade Mantea is still angry, but Lia isn't sure what to think of him. Afterwards Mother and Dad wanted to know exactly what he said. They didn't believe her that they talked about her drawings.

Comrade Mantea is staring into thin air. He looks like he is thinking very hard.

'We've grown numb. It's like this, kid: in wars, you have to face guns and cannons and soldiers, and the situation is somehow so obviously serious that we mobilise our courage, and our will, and so on. But here, we are supposed to be heroic at our kitchen table, at the factory, on the bus. We are supposed to risk terrible consequences just for saying some perfectly commonsense thing. It never seems worth it.'

She's pretending to listen, but really she's thinking how lucky she is Comrade Mantea is her friend. He talks complete gibberish but it never feels like he's lying to her. He's nice to her, and he has ideas, not only about grown-up problems but about everyone's problems.

'I will get that letter, I promise,' she says. She says it again as he shows her out of the flat.

Later that day Lia is in the living room, drawing and thinking about the business of the letter. She'll have to do it in the first hour of the day – all the teachers will either be teaching or they won't be at school yet. At least, that's the plan. It would all be so much easier if stupid Cauliflower would just tell her what the stupid letter says.

She has never been inside the staffroom, but many times she caught glimpses of it from the doorway. The room smells of cigarette smoke and perfume. She remembers a corner with many pot plants, four desks with drawers, typewriters. A large metal cupboard. Where could the letter be?

Mother comes in then, looking exhausted. She has been cleaning out the pantry.

'Aren't you cold?' Mother says, even though she's the one shivering. She grabs a blanket and puts it around Lia's shoulders.

'What's this?' Mother asks.

Lia has been drawing their town, but the way it will be

once the Dear Leader makes the bad people return every last bit of colour. It will be perfect. The people on the street will be radiant and wearing bright clothes. The radiance is made up of rays around their heads, like the ones beaming from the heads of saints and angels in church.

For a moment Mother looks angry, and Lia can see she is thinking about the fish again, but then she wipes away a tear. She kisses the top of Lia's head. 'Oh God, I'm so tired,' Mother says, and hugs her hard. 'We'll get through this competition curse, don't worry. It'll be over soon. One way or another,' she says. 'Darling,' she holds Lia's face in front of her. 'Do you understand that your father and I, we'll go insane if something happens to you? We are so bad at talking about this! I mean, sometimes at night I replay the things we said to you in my head, and I'm ashamed at how it sounds. We sound so mean, somehow. But it's because we are afraid. Do you understand that?' She looks Lia in the eyes. 'And the main reason we are afraid is you. If something happens to me and Victor, you'll be alone. The two of you don't even have grandparents. It's a horrible enough thought to make a mother lose her mind.'

She hugs Lia tight; kisses her again.

'I am sorry, Comrade Teacher, but I really need to go to the bathroom!'

Lia, standing up in class, is holding her belly for good measure. There follows a very long moment of fear at what she's just said, fear that's like a drink with many tiny bubbles in it. She hardly hears the giggling of the classmates around her.

Comrade Sava makes her eyes small when she turns to her, but eventually the teacher points her finger at the door. Lia can leave.

When she steps out of the classroom the empty corridor is strangely silent. She walks towards the steps. The balustrade feels too wide for her hand, and too high up, something she's never noticed before. It's like the school is suddenly for giants. She keeps looking behind her.

You have to be brave, kid, she imagines Comrade Mantea saying. *We can't let the bad people win.*

She runs the last few metres. Upstairs, by the staffroom, her whole body is trembling as she touches the door handle.

It's unlocked.

She opens the door.

There's no one inside. Lia closes the door behind her. She looks around.

The room has a few filing cabinets in a corner, and four desks.

She tiptoes to the filing cabinets, every step or so checking behind her. She opens the first one. Comrade Mantea couldn't tell her where to look, or exactly what for. 'Do they have a filing system? Maybe it will be under "events"?' he said.

The folders are organised by class. All eight of them have their own section. There is a file that says 'Work Sheets', one that says 'Supply List', one 'Literature'. She backs off from the filing cabinets, tries to think. She goes to the desk that she's seen Comrade Sava at and opens one of the small drawers. There, under a diary, is a pile of typewritten papers. They must be important letters, they all have big black stamps. She takes them out one by one. The top one speaks about 'The Saving of Resources', then another one is about the elections and voting booths, and then she finds it! 'Regional Chalk-Drawing Competition for Pioneers'! She's just about to leave when she realises this is the letter that announced the competition. It isn't what Comrade Mantea needs.

She finally finds her letter at the bottom of the pile. 'Organisational Matters', it says. She stuffs it down her stockings and goes back to the class.

Lia is dying to give Comrade Mantea the letter, but she stops in her tracks in front of his door. There's something not right inside the flat. She presses her ear against the door: there's swearing, and loud noises as though stuff is being thrown around. Her hand hovers over the bell. *Come on, do something before some nosybody sees you,* she says to herself. She rings.

A moment's silence, then a rumbling as though a beast is throwing itself at the entrance. The door flies open.

'Don't look at me like that,' Comrade Mantea says after a moment's staring. He is breathing heavily, like he's been running. He looks even more messy than usual.

She wants to follow him in, but the hallway is like an obstacle course. A shoe cabinet is overturned in the middle. The clothes-rack lies flat on its back on the floor. Shoes, coats, hats in a jumble all around.

She manages to cross the hallway without stepping on Comrade Mantea's things. In the kitchen, more surprises: the cabinets that are on the floor have been dragged away from the wall, and the suspended ones are all open, their contents spread out on the kitchen table. Even the fridge has wandered to the middle of the room. The switches and sockets, something has happened to them as well: their covers have come off and she can see their cable-and-metal guts.

Comrade Mantea is rummaging among the things on the floor. Finally he finds what he was looking for – a toothpick – and sits down, thoughtfully picking his teeth. With his foot he pulls a stool from under the table for Lia to have a sit.

He looks exhausted.

She cranes her neck to see into the bedroom; yes, it looks like the whirlwind has been there as well.

'What happened?' she asks.

Comrade Mantea doesn't seem to hear her. He is looking towards the hallway. Suddenly he shoots up, drags a stool to the front door and climbs on it. There's a small metal box above the front door, which he opens. Lia remembers they have one at home as well: the 'electricity board'. Comrade Mantea shines a small flashlight into the little box, mutters to himself. After a few minutes he returns to the kitchen.

'I could have bet my life,' he says, to himself. Then he turns to her. 'Maybe they're not so diligent. Not so clever!' he says and taps the side of his forehead.

He explains that he has made this entire mess himself. He is looking for hidden microphones. Not the singing microphones, the small ones that bad people use for listening. He thinks they may have been eavesdropping on them talking. Because of their big secret.

'Really?' she whispers. She tries to imagine someone listening

159

to them on a radio, but she cannot picture a person, only a shadow.

Comrade Mantea seems upset again. He keeps running his hands through his hair, and madly looking around.

'No! I can't just assume it's fine, there's too much at stake.' He stands up and starts pacing the kitchen, just kicking stuff out of the way. He stops in the middle, under the naked light-bulb, with his hands holding his head.

'Oink oink,' Lia says loudly. 'Oink oink oink oink!'

Comrade Mantea looks at her as though she's mad.

She laughs. 'Auuuuuuuu,' she then howls like a wolf towards the kitchen ceiling. 'Auuuuuuuuu!' It is strangely wonderful to do this. Howling! Indoors!

Comrade Mantea lets his hands fall. He smiles! She is laughing through her howling.

Suddenly he tenses, puts his elbows up like a bird and starts making chicken noises: 'Squawk squawk squawk squawk squawk!' in a high-pitched woman's voice, tiptoeing with his elbows flapping around the kitchen disaster. He even moves like a chicken, the sudden pauses and the pulling back of the head. She has never seen anything funnier. 'Auuuuuuuu!' she goes to keep him company, and they keep it up until they both double up with laughter. Comrade Mantea collapses on to the chair. 'Yeah, that should show them if they're listening.' He wipes away tears.

She catches a glimpse then of the clock, and sees that Mother will be home in fifteen minutes.

'Here!' she says, and hands him the letter.

Comrade Mantea whistles out loud as he takes the paper, then stands up and kisses the top of her head.

But he seems less and less pleased as he reads the letter.

'It's the letter,' Lia says. 'From the Mayor.'

Comrade Mantea says, 'Yeah. I was hoping there would be more detail. This was really the only letter?'

She nods.

'Well, we know one thing: you'll be riding in an open-top car that will pick you up from the Town Hall and take you to the stadium, and there you will say your silly poems. I suspect the Dear Leader will be with you in the car, else why bother to put you in an open-top car? They're just trying to keep his whereabouts a secret.'

Comrade Mantea looks around the kitchen, at the mess of displaced furniture, empty bottles and dirty dishes.

'Right. Our project has moved to the next stage,' Comrade Mantea says.

Lia looks at the clock again. This is so exciting, but she has to leave.

'Mother is being very annoying, I have to tell her where I am every minute. Someone told her they'd seen me in your block.'

'Really?'

'I said I came to listen to the neighbours' bear meetings.'

'Well, that was clever of you.'

She shrugs. 'It's terrible. Mother is always afraid of something.'

Comrade Mantea swigs back a shot of smelly drink. He looks at Lia. 'I was going to give you another master-spy task.'

She claps her hands. 'Give me, give me!' The school spy mission was the most fun she's had in ages.

'But it involves you being away from home for about an

hour. How will you manage that if your parents won't let you out of their sight?'

'I'll come up with something. I'm here now, aren't I?'

He covers his face with his hand. 'Damn stupid of me to arrange it without checking with the kid first,' he says to himself.

'But I can do it! What is it?'

'It's like this: I have a railroad engineer friend who has . . . let's say an ingredient that we need for our present. He is travelling around the country for work but he will be here on Sunday, until two, for an engine repair. After that he won't be back until after the Dear Leader's visit. And the ingredient, well, it's not something that can be put in the post. Railroad works, you understand?' He taps the side of his nose. 'We don't want to raise suspicions.'

She apes him and taps the side of her nose.

'He's a bit antsy about doing it, but I told him a kid would pick up the parcel. It's the least risky. Parents and grandparents send food parcels by train all the time.'

'That's it? Picking up a parcel?'

'From the railway station, from engineer Rădescu.'

She is disappointed.

'Do you think now,' he adds, 'could it be possible, if it's not too much to ask, think of it as my advance birthday and Christmas present, that you please just do this tiny thing I asked you and not try to topple the goddamn government in the process?'

She giggles.

'But seriously now,' he says. 'I've been meaning to ask you something.'

He looks at her as if she's a grown-up. He puts his elbows on the table and brings his hands together. 'Lia.'

'I can get the parcel,' she says.

He waves a hand. 'It's not that.' He fiddles with the collar of his bathrobe while staring into thin air. He sighs. When he finally speaks, it's in a sad voice.

'I need you to understand that this gift thing could be dangerous. They might get upset. With the likes of the Dear Leader, you can never know. People have been thrown in jail, or worse, for far less. Are you still prepared to do it? If it's really, really dangerous?' He slaps a hand on the table. 'Oh, how can I explain it to you? I mean – it could be painful. Look here' – he points at her up and down – 'you always have some scab or bruise from whatever devilry you're up to. Imagine now, this hurt could be a lot worse. We will be heroes, yes, but do you agree it's worth it? This risk that something bad might happen?'

He is suddenly sounding like Mother, Dad and Cauliflower all in one. Afraid.

'Lia. What do we do?' he asks. 'Do we go ahead with this, or not?'

Lia looks down at her legs. He's right, there are four long scabs on her shin from trying to wash a stray cat under a street tap.

'The terrible thing is,' he goes on, 'it's not as if we can ask anyone for advice. We have to trust our own minds.' He jabs at the side of his forehead.

'But we won't get caught. And we are doing something nice,' she says. The orange cat, it did not want to be washed, but this is different. Everybody likes colours. 'They're not going to punish us when they see that.'

He nods gravely. 'You are a very brave child. I couldn't have chosen a better partner.'

When she's at the door, just before she leaves, he says, 'Truth be told I know exactly what your poor mother feels like. We're both worried sick that you'll do something bonkers.' He taps her shoulder. 'Sunday, yes? He'll be there until two. If for some reason you can't make it, come and tell me and I'll go myself – he'll be furious but we can't miss him. There's no one else who can get us this thing.'

9

Piteşti, July

In his dream he is in a strange new town, some completely unknown place, and he and everyone else in this town are looking for Fram the circus bear in sheds and under cars, in garages and dead-end alleys, but they've only found the bear's shadow. The shadow is much, much bigger than Fram; a bear-shaped soot stain across roads and tower blocks and hills. But everyone in the town is still looking for Fram, as if nothing were amiss with this state of things.

When he wakes he remembers he has to hurry to his court date. He's a witness in a manslaughter case, the state versus a factory worker. The accused woman left her two children alone at home during her night shift and found them asphyxiated in the morning. The prosecution claims that she forgot the gas was on. Constantin was the one called to the scene at the time, and knows what happened: it had been December, minus twelve degrees outside, and the heating was off all over town. The kids must have turned on the gas stove to get warm and gone to bed. But sometimes the town cuts off the gas as well, not just the heating, so the fire went out. And when the gas came back on again, the kids were fast asleep.

Murdered by the national energy saving targets.

He was supposed to interrogate her, but instead this woman became the only one he has talked to, or tried talking to, about his own loss. He still doesn't know why he thought it would help, in that situation, to tell her about someone else's dead child, but he felt that her circumstances, having to go to work and leave her children unsupervised overnight, were comparable to his; she would understand the business of terrible choices. Or maybe he just knew that she was so deep inside her own sorrow that she would hardly hear him. He told her, when my daughter fell ill, they offered me a solution. You see, they thought they were being kind. They said, there are benefits to being a police officer, to being a pillar of the state. You'll wait for a suitable donor for as long as reasonably possible, but if nothing comes up, we'll do what is necessary. The country is full of abandoned, wretched kids, cripples with no present and a short, miserable future. Of course we must save a child who is otherwise healthy, with loving parents. He told this woman, I loved my daughter more than anything but I couldn't do it.

The woman never asked, 'Then why . . . ?' She never said anything.

'The gas pipe was corroded, your honour,' he says in court, 'it happens sometimes. Machinery is not infallible.' He explains from the witness stand how it was nobody's fault, or everybody's fault – at this, the judge eyes him menacingly – and that the state should not further punish someone already so unfortunate.

Throughout the proceedings the accused stares blankly ahead. She will not help him help her.

But the judge also seems to want to let the poor woman go and does not seriously challenge his lies. After she delivers her 'innocent' verdict they have a cup of real coffee in her office. Constantin savours his with his eyes closed. When he opens them, he finds the judge looking at him.

'Justice has to suffer many indignities on this earth,' she sighs.

He nods back. 'At least,' he says, 'today we didn't add to Lady Justice's woes.'

She looks away, muttering, 'Filthy business,' into her cup.

'How are you coping?' he asks.

What has flown into him?

But he finds himself insisting, 'How many times a day do you bite your tongue?'

The judge looks at him. He can see her weighing her options. *Is he Securitate? Is he insane?*

Thinking, thinking.

He, too, is holding his breath. Did he just manage to get himself reported?

'Sometimes I wish I were too stupid to keep count,' she finally says.

It's nothing, just a judge allowing herself a moment's candour, but he leaves the courthouse elated.

On his way back to the station he stops at an army roadblock; they've popped up everywhere, even in town centres. A young soldier holding a huge, shaggy dog on a short lead approaches the car in front of Constantin. The dog leaps up against the car door; a woman screams from inside. Annoyed, the soldier yanks the dog off the car, but the animal keeps pulling. The driver is an elderly woman, and eventually it becomes clear that she has an ancient pistol in her handbag – the dog is probably sensing the gunpowder. Constantin feels deeply uncomfortable watching the woman beg the soldiers to let her keep the weapon. 'I would only use it on myself!' she wails.

There's a madness in the air since the bear. Everybody is that tiny bit less sane. He thinks about the judge's words: *I wish I were stupid*. He knows what she meant. A stupid man wouldn't feel guilty for pretending that the killer is a bear. He wouldn't know or care that because of this lie, people are on their guard for a bear, not a human killer. That people are opening their doors to the human killer.

In the office he finds Vasile slumped at his desk, with a pile of files in front of him. For the last three days both Constantin and his constable have been reading the handwritten reports that are the initial sources for each bear victim's Securitate file.

Six of the regional Securitate offices replied and confirmed that the victims were indeed informers. Eight others said that the information is classified and needs Minister-level approval, and the rest have not replied yet. But Constantin is certain now that all the victims were informers. That has to be the common denominator. The only problem is that he still hasn't found the information that allows the killer to attack his victims when they are alone and vulnerable. It does not seem to exist in the reports. It's frustrating beyond belief – as though he has found not an actual smoking gun, but just the smoke.

Davidescu comes up to his desk. The police chief looks as if he had a rough night. He is unshaven and his little pig eyes are red and irritated.

'Anything new?'

Constantin shakes his head.

Davidescu closes his eyes; huffs. 'I've got half a mind to go and get some drunkard and beat him up until he not only signs a confession, he believes it himself that he's a fucking bear.'

Constantin must have looked alarmed because Davidescu waves a hand. He was just venting.

'We could do a lot more in terms of warning the population,' Constantin says. 'They're the ones dying, after all.'

'Haven't you noticed?' Davidescu says. 'Nobody gives a shit.'

And nobody is happier than you about that, Constantin wants to say. 'That's not true,' he says instead. 'They've just stopped talking about it on the news.'

Davidescu is right in that sense: they've stopped announcing the killings, stopped mentioning victims. The other day Sandu sat patiently through the news and when they reached the end yet again without mention of the case, the boy looked at him and said proudly, *Daddy caught the bear.*

'They stopped putting it on the news because it's all the same whether they go on about it or not,' Davidescu says. 'And after all, it's only twenty dead people out of twenty million. We're losing more than that to wasps.'

'I had two cases of death by tyre,' Vasile says. 'You know, tyres coming off lorries at full speed? The car mechanic doesn't fix them screws properly, and boom. If it happens anywhere busy it's like tenpin bowling.'

Constantin takes a deep breath.

'These warnings that you want,' Davidescu says, as he walks away, 'they'll just make it painfully clear that we have no fucking clue.'

'Are these informer people paid by the number of words?' Vasile suddenly says. 'I'm going crazy here. Two pages of gibberish for every line that makes it into the final report.'

Vasile has been complaining non-stop since he started going through the pile. 'Pages and pages of some stupid housewife's boring diary.' In a fake high-pitched voice, he reads from one of the files, 'On Wednesdays I always make my husband's favourite dessert, "bird milk", and as it requires a fair bit of whisking – you cannot decently put it on the table before the foam is hard, it needs to be almost like mash – I just put eggs, milk and everything on the windowsill and do the whisking there, and it's all the better for watching everyone, and also I can forget my arm hurts from all the whisking. It's a good hour for watching the street . . .'

Vasile looks pleadingly up at Constantin.

But Constantin feels as though time stops. He forgets to breathe. He reaches out for a file. Vasile stops him. 'No, that one's almost normal. Take this one.' He hands him a file, opens it at the first page. Constantin reads, 'I was at my son's football game the other day, I make a point to go to every game, it doesn't matter that he's only six. It's good education for the kids, good exercise, we want healthy kids who can stand up for themselves. I was an athlete myself, went to three national competitions. You wouldn't guess it if you knew my weight now but ten years ago I could still get a place on any national league rugby team. Anyway, at that football game last week I hear Comrade Stoenescu say to his son that if he scores he'll get him Coca-Cola. Where would he get Coca-Cola from? In May? We see it in December and even then . . .'

Vasile nods slowly. 'You see?'

Constantin tries to stay calm, not letting his voice betray his excitement. 'We're looking in the wrong place. Call our special friends, please, and ask them for the source reports written by the victims themselves. Not the ones *about* them. The ones *by* them.'

Vasile stops for a moment, does the maths. 'That's even more reports than this lot!' he points at the piles in front of him.

'Tough. I want them yesterday!' Constantin says. He leaves the office calmly enough, only to then run the two kilometres to the university. He hurls himself down the steps to Titus's office, pushing aside seasick-looking students.

'It'll all be there, I'm sure. All the necessary clues,' he says to Titus, demented Norwegian trolls marching in the background. The coroner is still looking at the sample reports that Constantin brought.

'Who knew?' Titus mutters. 'So many aspiring essayists in our country. Little Montaignes, the lot of them.'

Constantin shrugs. 'It's like they are lonely. They want to tell someone about themselves.' Then, 'But you agree, no? It's exactly the kind of stuff that would be useful to someone wanting to find these people on their own.'

'We have all been snitching on ourselves,' Titus says. 'Literally.'

'It's a good hunch, right? I'm not going crazy?' Constantin asks again. He sounds just like Sandu, he thinks, seeking reassurance about something good that is going to happen.

Titus nods. 'If you're right, then the next question is, do they keep a log of some kind? For accessing the local archives.'

'I've not been there, we had everything sent to us. I need to check. If there's a log . . . we've got him. By God, we've got him. We only need the same name to pop up in a few of the towns.'

'I wonder if we actually have some kind of deranged hero on our hands,' Titus says. He raises an eyebrow. 'Don't give me that look. He is killing informers. Nothing but informers.'

Constantin has thought about this, too. 'I still think it's convenience. He has access to this information. I can't imagine that someone who is anti-system would choose to fight the system in this way.'

'Sometimes you're like a child,' Titus says. 'You think there's good and evil, and that they're like two elegant tennis players each sticking to the rules in their respective halves.'

'They're not?' Constantin says, pressing the button to finally silence the devilish music.

It takes two weeks for Securitate to comply with the request, but eventually Constantin receives the reports. His hands start trembling when he finds the relevant passage. He leans forwards on the desk, puts the file down and folds his arms so that Vasile doesn't notice his excitement. *You see, I like to think about things like that. I'm someone who takes the time to think about things like that. About being careful, about doing things properly. Every Sunday morning I walk the eight kilometres to Gheoal Lake to fish, this time of year it's still dark and there's no one along the way, so a man can be alone with his thoughts. Some of my best ideas come then.*

These are the words of the first bear victim that Constantin came across. These torn-out pages of lined school notebook have once been held by the killer, Constantin is sure of that now. They're so close to catching him. They know twenty-three places where the killer has been, where people must have seen him. There's no chance that the bear will have passed unobserved or unremembered in all of them.

Vasile brought back some bad news as well: there's no log at the local archives. *You sign for entering the building if you're a visitor, but access to the archives is for agents only, and they don't have to sign in.* But this small impediment is nothing, nothing at all, compared to the certainty that they know where the killer has been. How he finds his victims.

Tomorrow, Constantin plans to take the train to Braşov, the last city where they had an attack, and speak to everyone who has been working at the archives in the past few weeks. It's been only four days since the murder, they will remember visitors. Especially since it's highly likely the visitor will have been from out of town.

'Have you heard of the Carpathian grizzlies?'

Davidescu has appeared in front of him. Constantin puts the file away, looks innocent. But he's already made up his mind to speak to the police chief today. Even for someone so reluctant to stick his neck out as him, not acting on this evidence will be very difficult.

'Listen to this,' Davidescu pulls up a chair so he sits in front of him. He leans in over the desk and starts whispering. 'As we all know,' the police chief says, 'Comrade Ceaușescu is very fond of hunting. The bigger the beast, the better. When he found out that American bears are much bigger than ours, he couldn't stand the thought that here he is hunting some kind of pygmy bear while the Yankees are having fun with the real thing. So he flew in a few dozen grizzlies and dropped them off all over the place, the idea being that they would just join the other animals and cavort happily until shot by Comrade Ceaușescu.' Davidescu tilts his head to one side and makes a disappointed face. 'This was about ten years ago. The imported grizzlies killed everything. Other bears, cattle, sheep, boar, wolves, horses, people; it was as if we had planted dinosaurs among normal-sized animals. The leadership realised fairly soon that they'd have to get rid of the monsters or our forests would be left with nothing bigger than mice.'

Constantin has been listening to the story without really paying attention, just waiting for Davidescu to come out with whatever he wants from him.

'We have been informed that Comrade Ceaușescu is concerned that one of these beasts has escaped after all. Maybe an enemy of the state stole it, and plans to use the animal for something much worse. We know these animals can be trained. You see, the ease with which it kills . . . and the fact that Comrade Ceaușescu is often out hunting and thus is vulnerable to bears.'

'What does this have to do with me?' Constantin asks.

Davidescu waves a hand. 'I know, it's nonsense. The really

interesting thing is – what will you say to Comrade Ceauşescu when he tells you his theory? I would pay good money to be a fly on that wall.'

'What?' Constantin says.

'The President wants to speak to our chief bear investigator himself. To see where we're at. To discuss this new lead about the grizzlies. To understand why there has been no progress for so long.' Davidescu turns to the office. 'Our little rebel here is about to learn to be very diplomatic indeed.'

Constantin waits for a punchline, but Davidescu is serious. He shows Constantin a fax from the presidency. It says they will come and pick him up tomorrow.

'We're joking here,' Davidescu says, 'but if anything comes out of your mouth that reflects badly on me or on this station, I will personally feed you to the police dogs. Oh, and I strongly advise you to present a suspect. Comrade President will not like it one bit that after all this time you've got nothing to go on.'

It's four p.m. and he and Titus are in a neighbourhood boozer. There are only three other customers. Constantin is having a beer while Titus has almost finished the small bottle of vodka that he ordered. 'Why beat around the bush?' Titus said when he ordered his drink.

Constantin looks around. He's been in places like this rounding up suspects: it is dark and filthy, sticky somehow. There's no music, only traffic noise. They're at a crossroads with the town's main road, and so a lot of cars, trucks and motorcycles stop and start just by its entrance; the smell is of stale alcohol and petrol. The other three punters look as if they are made of the same grime as the rest of the place. Two of them were arguing and swearing loudly when Constantin and Titus came in; the owner has been over to their table under the pretext of wiping it clean and, Constantin is sure, has told them he's a police officer. Since then they've been quiet and sullen. They look unhappily sober.

Constantin has given the coroner the good news about the informers' reports, the moderately bad news about a lack of any record for who accessed the archive, and the very bad news of being sent to the presidential summer palace. It was Titus who suggested they have a drink.

'Davidescu is right, you'll be in trouble if you don't give them something. A plan to catch the killer, another suspect . . .' Titus says. 'You could even tell them the truth. That it's someone in the secret services.'

Constantin shakes his head. 'They will bury it if they can. If it's just a vague suspicion against someone in the services, they will bury it. Once we have a name it will be much easier to get them to sacrifice one of their own.'

Titus suddenly looks worried. 'Actually, it's such a crazy excuse, to take you there because of this grizzly story . . . What if our killer is up to something?'

'What?'

'The killer could be someone high up in Securitate. Someone who can whisper in the president's ear that he should summon you.'

'Come on. They don't know we're on to them.'

'Eh, don't be stupid. Your boss asked all these local Securitate branches if the victims were informers. It's entirely plausible that they reported his snooping around.'

'Someone high up in Securitate can get to me without this grizzly nonsense, and definitely without involving the president. No. They don't know. If the killer does have anything to do with this invite, it's to see what we've got so far.'

'Please be careful,' Titus says.

Constantin laughs bitterly and empties his beer.

Titus looks intently at him. 'I want to tell you something but I'm afraid you're too damn . . .' and he makes a frustrated gesture with both hands, something suggesting a twisted ball of yarn.

'The day is pretty bad already, so go ahead.'

'My wife is always on a diet, God knows why. Ever since we met she's been on a diet.'

'She's . . . very thin.' Constantin has seen her once or twice, at official events. He remembers an anxious-looking woman with a ponytail.

'The ideal citizen, right? There would be no queues if only everyone was like her. The government could get away with providing nothing but air.'

Constantin is wondering where he's going with this.

Titus waves an arm, 'Actually I'm talking rubbish, Maria loves queueing, jabbers about food all the time. What I want to say is' – he points an accusing finger at Constantin – 'she has no notion of how much food is enough. How much is too little. We've got nerve receptors in the stomach, you know, but the other end goes into the brain, and if your brain is the kind that likes to decide things by itself, figure life out in the privacy of its folds and lobes and fluids, it can completely disable the end that has some actual contact with reality. Buggers it up well and good.'

Constantin feels an uncomfortable heat rising, all the way up to his ears. When he thinks someone means to speak about Alina, the first thing that happens is that his mind shuts down, does a 'this far and no further' on him.

Titus has a long look at him, then stands up and fetches another small transparent bottle from the bar. 'You'll follow my drift better.'

Titus pours him a glass.

There are three categories of people, Constantin believes: corrupt, intact, and too stupid – and he has put exactly no one in the intact column, it's pristine. There are football stadiums of people in the corrupt and too stupid columns. But where is Titus? What trick did Titus pull that makes him unclassifiable? Most importantly, why can't Constantin recuse himself like that?

'This thing that my wife is doing with food,' Titus says, 'this confusion about how much is enough, you're doing it with your notions of integrity.'

'I tried everything humanly decent!' Constantin finds himself shouting. He tried everything to save Alina, everything that wouldn't make a monster out of all of them.

'Calm down. I don't want to talk about that. I'm talking about this trip.'

Constantin empties his glass in one go and slams it on the table. The three drunkards are unashamedly staring at them.

'Your priority has to be to come back in one piece. For your family, for yourself. Whatever you see and hear there will be much worse than you expect, but you have to resist the temptation to make a martyr of yourself. It benefits no one. No one will hold survival against you. You shouldn't either.'

'But do you understand?' Constantin asks. The alcohol has gone to his head. He wants to say something about being good. How can he explain it? It can't be possible that people are supposed to be good only when it's easy to do so.

'We've ended up in this . . .' Constantin looks around at the red, puffed-up faces that have decided he's the afternoon's entertainment, at the shabby, unloved air of every single thing '. . . we've ended up in this cut-price hell because we were only too happy to look the other way.'

'All that is way above your pay grade, my friend. You've not been left in charge of life and the universe. Stop acting as if you were.'

They finish their drinks in silence. Constantin is trying to think beyond the Ceaușescu assignment. He tries to picture himself walking back through the door of his home. Maybe it's all right that this is happening. Maybe he can use this meeting to advance the investigation. Maybe he can obtain some special authority to force the Securitate to reveal the name of the person who accessed the archives all over the country. If anyone does have that info.

Maybe he's drunk.

'Titus? What if it's really not human?'

'The killer?'

'The killer.'

'You mean, that it actually is a very aggressive and clever bear?'

He thinks. 'I mean, what if it's exactly what we told the people? A beast, unstoppable. Evil manifest. Our own cursed evil.'

Titus empties the last drops of the vodka bottle. He grimaces, and looks at the label. 'I've stored bladders in better alcohol.'

When he arrives home he finds Tina in the kitchen, and an old love song playing on the radio. It's a 1930s recording with that distant, tinny sound and a voice that you know is long gone. He watches her from the doorway. She is standing with her back to him, by the window, swaying slightly. Her right hand hovers above the radio, as if she were in the process of switching it off but is being kept at bay by the music.

It would be a good moment to make a start, he thinks, to take her in his arms and kiss her neck. He steps into the kitchen. But her hand comes down on the radio just then and kills the music. He's disappointed, though he knows she's right: the best thing he can do for her and Sandu at this point is to prepare for his meeting. Find a plausible lead. *I would strongly advise you to present a suspect.*

He retreats to the bedroom, his arms full of notebooks. He will just go through everything again.

Little lies, he thinks. Everything bad must have started like that, innocently, with small untruths that people thought did not matter in the greater scheme of things. Even people who were uncomfortable with the small lies didn't protest, because, after all, they were small and it seemed of great importance to others that these lies pass. He can see himself, in the midst of some heated discussion, worrying that it's unkind, obstinate even, to point out that surely, if some great and worthy end justifies the means, then this end would not be at risk from something as neutral as the truth.

And now: eternal fog. Bears. Dictators. Human crimes blamed on animals.

He is almost asleep at the desk by the time Sandu opens the door and says, 'Daddy, you forgot.' He had not forgotten, but he knows Sandu will not like tonight's story.

Constantin opens his arm and waits for the boy to snuggle in. 'Some stories are more difficult, and not much fun when you first hear them, but they are a bit like the greens that you don't like to eat. The spinach is good for your body, and the green stories are good for your soul.'

The boy looks disappointed. 'No princes tonight,' he says, a serious look on his face.

Constantin kisses the top of his head. 'No princes.'

He opens the notebook.

'There was once a faraway land with earth that was mostly barren and waters in which fishes did not thrive. For the poor people living there, making the ground yield something edible was akin to squeezing blood from a stone, but this mean land was not the end of their troubles. Every autumn, locust swarms fell upon the land and ate everything they had worked so hard to grow. More often than not the peasants were left with roots and summer apples, the carcasses of the animals that had starved to death, and the sour, unripe fruit they had picked and stowed away before the swarms.

'The legend goes that somewhere in the midst of this country was a little village that year after year was spared the misery of the locusts. How so, you may ask? Well, many lifetimes ago, a great wizard had passed through the village. He'd asked for lodgings and a meal, and at first he had been disappointed with what the villagers put on the table. Dry rusks, a bit of cheese, small, withered apples, and spring water instead of wine. But the wizard, who could see through walls, saw that the family that had taken him in had emptied their larder for him. In other places he had been offered a slightly better meal, but the hosts had always hidden away the best morsels. Impressed with the decency and generosity he had encountered, the wizard gave these poor people a fistful of tiny red seeds. "Scatter them around your village," he said. "It is the Shame Flower. It will grow red for as long as the people of this village have shame. The locusts will see it and be so ashamed by their own greed, they will have to turn away from the sight."

'The villagers did as he told them, and soon these flowers, red with the thinnest of white edges, enclosed the village in a red ring. In the years that followed, autumn after autumn, the locust swarms darkened the horizon. The dark cloud hovered for a moment in the distance, and then it was as if the wind turned and blew it away, for the cloud never again descended on the village.'

Maybe he could have been a hero, Constantin thinks, if heroic opportunities had presented themselves. He could have mustered courage for the big moments. But no: little cuts, death by little cuts. The problem is, if you make a fuss over the small things, you appear insane, and if you wait until they try to pull the big things over you, by then it's too late. They'll ask, well, why didn't you say something before? Why did you wait until the absurdity of a serial killer bear?

'Daddy,' Sandu pokes his side.

'Yes, sorry. The villagers became fatter and wealthier. And through the years, so slowly that hardly anyone noticed, the white edge of the flowers became wider, and the red shrank towards the middle. The villagers had begun to change their ways: visitors were given the thinnest, smelliest straw mattresses to sleep on, and the best food was kept under lock in the larder. People went back on their word, lying to their friends and neighbours. Husbands and wives had affairs, and children waited for their parents to be out of the house so they could steal some coins. Flowers from fresh graves were stolen to be sold again at the market.

'Some of the elders noticed the shrinking red centre, and one Sunday in church the priest talked to his parishioners about it. He reminded them of the locust swarms and of the wizard's words. He spoke, trying not to offend anyone, of deeds that might have caused the flowers to whiten. But none of the villagers felt it had anything to do with them.

'One year, before the regional fair, the villagers had force-fed their sheep so much salt that the poor animals drank whole buckets of water, and weighed in at much more than their real weight. The villagers returned home with heavy purses, and boasted to their wives about how they had tricked their customers. That autumn, for the first time, the flowers had more white than red.

'The year after that the locusts hovered for many minutes over the village before they turned away, and for the first time the villagers watched the buzzing dark cloud from their court-yards and feared for their crops again. But then the cloud lifted and even the ones who had some shred of shame left saw their neighbours' behaviour, and felt that it would be foolish of them to be the only honest folk in a dishonest village.

'And so the next year the locusts came. And the locusts ate and ate; they ate for all the years they hadn't fed on this village, until they had eaten even the clothes on the villagers' backs, and the villagers tried to cover their private parts with their hands, averting their eyes from each other's nakedness, and that was the first time that year that any of them had felt a little shame.'

Sandu looks up at him when he finishes. The boy giggled a little at the nakedness part, but on the whole the story seems to have made him uneasy.

Some stories just are like that.

10

Sighișoara, July

It's Monday evening, and there's another blackout. Mother and Dad are whispering about work by the light of the oil lamp. Dani is playing under the kitchen table.

Lia decides to take revenge on Comrade Cauliflower by redoing the destroyed outer space drawing exactly the way it's supposed to be. She puts the crayons and the drawing book on the washing machine, where the oil lamp is, and pulls her chair there too. But her knees have nowhere to go, and when she bumps them against the wonky washing machine, the lamp topples on the back of her hand. Lia watches the oil run across her fingers.

The next thing she knows, Mother lunges at her, pulling her away from the flames. Dad throws a cloth and the small fire is put out.

When Lia looks at her hand she sees that a long strip of skin has curled up like the jerky they have at Christmas. It's only then that she realises she's in pain. Bad, bad pain. She screams. Mother and Dad turn the kitchen sink tap on and off, shouting at each other over whether or not they should douse her hand in water. Dad wraps her in a blanket, picks her up and rings a neighbour to ask if he has petrol in his car and if Dad could borrow it to drive to the hospital.

Lia falls asleep during the long wait in the hallways. When she wakes up she finds her hand huge and white in a bandage. It's very late when they return home. In bed, under Mother's arm, she's still crying.

'It's all Cauliflower's fault,' she sobs.

'Shh,' Mother says, stroking her hair.

The next morning there is cocoa and pancakes with prune jam for breakfast. Mother and Dad make a fuss over her. She realises that today she's a Victim, and no one is allowed to be angry at her. With her mouth full of pancake, Lia goes to the hallway and gets the little red grade book out of her backpack. Mother or Dad need to sign all her grades as soon as Comrade Sava puts a new one in the book, but Lia hasn't shown it to them for weeks. Sava has been very mean lately.

Dad just shakes his head at her when he reads the last entry. Mother asks 'What?' but Dad puts a hand on Mother's shoulder and that's it.

The following day, at special classes, Lia thinks that the teacher will ask about her huge bandaged hand, but Sava just takes one hard look at it and says, 'God help your poor parents.' Then they go through the usual anthems and poems and history, and Lia lets her thoughts wander. The wandering cannot be seen on her face, but still, she wakes up to Sava shouting, 'Do you hear me? Anything you say or do that is not something we discussed here can get your parents taken away and put in prison. Surely, even a troublesome child like you can understand that?'

This is new. And pretty rotten. Everybody has been telling her what to say and what not to say, but that still left a lot of possibilities. There were still all the things she hasn't specifically been told not to say.

'Check with your parents if you don't believe me,' the teacher goes on. 'If you forget a line in a poem, that's going to be bad, but it's nothing compared to what will happen if you say any of the appallingly seditious stuff that routinely comes out of your mouth.'

'Seditious?' Lia says. What does that even mean?

'Everything! All of it! Every single thought in your head!'

Sava falls back in her chair, red in the face from shouting.

On her way home, Lia thinks about Cauliflower's words. Could it be true? She has caught grown-ups making threats that they don't really mean, many times. When Lia was smaller, Mother used to tell her she would give her away to the gypsies if she didn't behave, and Mother still frightens Dani with that sometimes. But she's saying it only for the scare.

At home, Lia turns on the television until Mother and Dad come back from work. Really she just means to sit there and stare at the TV, maybe cry a little because on the whole it has been such a bad week, and if she thinks about it her left hand hurts, but the film they are playing on the TV pulls her in. The story is about a class of teenagers who are angry at their government. There is also a war going on. A young man becomes the leader of this class of upset teenagers. He talks them into fighting against the bad people. One night they break into a factory that makes weapons, and they set it on fire. Throughout the film there is a lot of talk about something called 'pamphlets'. The teenagers let these pamphlet things fly from rooftops or leave them at bus stops on the benches.

The film is so good Lia doesn't hear when Mother returns from work. She just notices Mother standing in the living room.

'It's a very good film,' Lia says. 'What's a pamphlet?'

'I've seen this one,' Mother says. She looks pleased. 'The workers were oppressed by fascists and capitalists, so these brave youngsters spread their ideas by publishing pamphlets. It means leaflet, or booklet. They wrote down what they were upset about, usually the fascist government, and the horrible things the fascists were doing. They tried to convince everyone else to join them in their fight.'

'These men in uniform are fascists? They are very bad,' Lia says.

'Yes, fascists are terrible people.'

'And this happened for real?'

'Yes. Many years ago.'

'Was I born?'

'No, silly, during the Second World War.'

Lia sees an imaginary ruler before her eyes, with five nicks at even intervals: Dinosaurs, Romans, Turks, World Wars, Lia.

'And they won? It worked?'

'Of course it worked. Do you see any fascists around here?' Mother laughs.

'This is a very good film,' Lia says. Mother comes over and pats her on the head.

By the end of the film, many people have read the pamphlets and come around to the cause of the teenagers. Everyone celebrates the end of the war and victory over the fascists.

Lia climbs down from the sofa and turns off the TV. She goes into the kitchen, through the hallway so as not to disturb Mother and Dad, who are having their afternoon nap.

She gets out the calligraphy notebook and a black crayon. From the middle of the notebook she tears out three double pages. She holds them against the side of the table with her bad hand and with the good hand she tears them in half, and half again. She ends up with twelve pieces of paper about the size of playing cards. She uses big capital letters, and ends with a fat exclamation mark that looks like a chicken drumstick. She does this twelve times, then she folds the pamphlets until they are the size of a stamp.

When Mother and Dad wake up she begs them to let her out.

'You'll manage to fall and injure your hand,' Dad says.

'I'll just sit on a bench. I promise. Half an hour. Please, a breath of fresh air?'

'*A breath of fresh air*,' Mother chortles. 'You little monkey. Don't ape us.'

They let her go. None of her friends are in the courtyard but it doesn't matter. She goes to the bench by the garden and leaves four of her pamphlets there, safe from the wind under a rock, and then she does the same thing on the bench in front of the blocks and the one next to the car park.

Everyone is in the kitchen when she gets back. Mother is preparing supper. Dad is making Dani laugh with funny faces.

She sits down, resting her bad hand on the kitchen table. Dad whispers into Dani's ear, 'Your sister is turning into a pirate. See, a hook's coming out of that bandaged stump. Then come the eye patch and the parrot.'

'Ha-ha,' Lia says, taking out her crayons from the drawer.

'Don't give this kid any ideas. She'll poke her eye out next,' Mother says.

Dad points at the crayons. 'To be honest, after the accident I'd have expected you to stay away from drawing paraphernalia for a while.'

'I've already used them today,' Lia says. 'For writing, not for drawing.'

'Oh, really? What did you write?'

'Mother knows,' she says.

Mother shrugs. 'I've no idea.'

'Yes, you do. The film,' Lia says.

'So show me what you've written,' Dad says.

'What film?' Mother asks.

'You know. The pamphlets.'

Mother turns to Lia, frowning. 'But I told you there are no fascists any more.'

Lia shrugs. 'There are other bad people.'

Dad looks at Mother. 'What's this about?'

Mother takes the frying pan off the stove. She sits on a chair next to Lia. 'Show me what you've written,' she says.

'I can't. I distributed them.' Lia is proud to use the new word she learned from the film.

Mother slaps Lia. Lia is so surprised that her face is still smiling seconds after the blow.

'What did you do with them?' Mother shakes her.

Her poor left hand then hits the side of the fridge; she screams. It's a nightmare – Mother is shaking her and shouting at her, and Dad, for the first time ever, is not trying to calm Mother down, but instead closes the kitchen window so the neighbours won't hear Lia's crying. She ends up lying on the floor. Everyone's faces are red, and Mother is crying, too. Dani has crawled into a corner. Lia feels that Mother and Dad do not understand, she herself does not understand, no one anywhere has ever understood anything. They keep shouting at her: 'What did you do with them? Where are they?'

The doorbell rings then. Mother and Dad stare at the end of the hallway as though the Devil himself is waiting there.

The doorbell rings again.

Dad pushes Mother aside and goes to the door. Lia hears whispering. Then the door closes and Dad comes back into the kitchen. He looks tired. Mother has her hand over her mouth. They look very old.

'It was your friend Popa,' Dad says. 'She saw her leave the papers. She suspected it might be trouble. She went to collect them before someone else did.'

Dad puts his head in his hands. Mother is crying again, this time quietly.

'We'll be all right,' he says. 'Nobody's seen them.'

Dad drops the crumpled pamphlets on the kitchen worktop and grabs the matchbox. He turns the tap on, lights a match and sets a bunch of them on fire in the sink. His hands are trembling.

'Victor . . .' Mother says. She has unfolded and read one of the pamphlets. She hands it to Dad. He seems not to believe what he is seeing.

Lia crawls under the kitchen table, hides as far back as possible.

Dad blows the match out and turns the tap off. His hands sink into his lap. He picks up another pamphlet, reads it, then another one, and Mother, too, until they have read all of them. He rests his head in his hands; they still tremble.

Mother is staring at Lia. She has nowhere to go from under the kitchen table. But Dani dares crawl out from his corner, approach the worktop and pull down a piece of paper. Mother and Dad let him. Dani looks at the paper.

'What does it say?' he asks.

Dad picks him up, sits him on his lap. He takes a deep breath. '"Astronaut!" All they say is "Astronaut!"'

'I hate them,' she says. She's in Comrade Mantea's kitchen, telling him about the pamphlet trouble the other day and about her burnt hand.

Comrade Mantea sighs. 'Kid. Look at me,' he knocks on the table. 'I don't like your stupid parents any more than you do. But they're in a godawful difficult situation. They're not trying to be mean to you.'

'But why are they being mean, then?'

He shrugs. 'Isn't everything difficult? Look at you. The

height of my knees, practically.' She can't help chuckling at this. 'And still here you are, every second week bawling your eyes out in my kitchen. Bandaged! And you're a kid. Imagine when you grow up. You don't even have the excuse of being tiny and everyone else knocking you about. You'll have to admit to yourself that . . .'

He stops himself.

'That what?'

'Never mind that now. Just trust me on this. Your parents, complete and utter assholes though they may be, they love you and don't really want to be mean to you.' He bends forwards as he says this, until his nose is almost touching hers.

'Now,' he says. 'Back to our business. You haven't forgotten about tomorrow? Your parents will let you go to the station?'

Lia nods.

'We're almost there, kid.' He musses her hair. Then, 'Ah, wait – where do we hide the gift until you present it?' Comrade Mantea looks at her as if he's sizing her up.

'In my backpack?' Lia says.

'Hm, not sure.' He ponders for a moment. 'I know! How about you do something to your school backpack, decorate it in some lovely patriotic way so they let you bring it with you on the day. Sew the flag on to it, or something like that. Then we can make a false bottom and hide our present in there. What do you say?'

She likes the decorating idea so much that already that evening she is in her armchair with the backpack in her lap. 'I'm decorating my backpack,' she tells Mother and Dad. 'With our flag. So it'll be extra nice for the Dear Leader's visit.'

Mother thinks it's an excellent idea, and even starts talking about where they might find the three coloured fabric strips. 'Yellow is going to be very difficult,' she muses.

'We could just buy an actual flag, and cut it up,' Dad says.

Lia wakes up very early on Sunday; it's barely light outside. She listens for sounds from Mother and Dad's bedroom, but there's just Dad's snoring. Nothing to be done except to wait.

The plan is to tell Mother that she's going out to play, and then to sneak to the train station. They always let her out to play on Sunday morning. Except . . . she pulls the cover aside and runs to the window. She looks at the sky.

Not a cloud, not even one of those friendly sheep ones. They have to let her out.

Time passes slower than on Christmas morning. She has to stop herself from making noises to wake everyone up; it's no good if she gets Mother and Dad annoyed.

Finally she can hear movement in the other room. She flies to the bathroom to wash her face, drags Dani along as well, and by the time Mother and Dad enter the kitchen they are both sitting at the breakfast table.

'Oh, good mor— What plates are those?' Mother interrupts herself. 'That's not the breakfast plates.'

Lia knows, but she can't reach the proper breakfast plates. They were not supposed to notice.

'Someone must be very hungry.' Dad ruffles her hair again.

She takes big bites out of her fried egg. In the middle of breakfast she says, 'I'll go out to play after this,' and Mother and Dad don't even answer her. They don't care – the best possible situation.

The doorbell rings then. Lia follows Mother to the door. It's the ground-floor neighbour; she whispers something to Mother and then rushes back down the stairs.

'They're bringing chicken!' Mother closes the door. 'Now, at the grocer's.' She's excited.

'Silvia,' Dad says. 'We promised my boss we'd help him with the move. We said we'll be there at ten-thirty.'

'Lia can go,' Mother says.

'No!' Lia says. 'It's Sunday, I'm playing. I told you.'

'Well, that's tough, but you also want to eat, don't you?' Mother hands her money, the ration card and a canvas shopping bag.

Lia lets everything drop to the floor and starts sobbing.

'Jesus Christ, this kid,' Dad says.

Mother shakes her gently by the shoulders. 'Listen – we'll be back in two hours. All right? Two hours, do you hear me? You can play the rest of the day.'

Between cry-hiccups Lia tries to think. It's nine-thirty now. Comrade Mantea said the train station man will be there until two. She'll be there in time if she leaves at twelve. It takes her something like twenty minutes to get there if she runs.

She weakly accepts the bag and everything else. Mother wipes the milk off the corners of her mouth with her apron. She shakes a finger at her. 'Don't you dare leave that queue before we get there.'

'Maybe you'll be lucky and you'll have the chicken by then,' Dad says.

Lia runs to the grocer's. She walks past the long line that stretches outside the shop. She counts forty-seven people. They are shouting back and forth in the queue, some rumours saying the chicken truck is around the corner, some that it's not due for hours. The shop entrance is still locked, and there's no one official to ask. She looks at her watch: it's ten.

Lia goes to the rear of the queue. Forty-seven people ahead of her is not so bad. If the chicken truck pulls up soon she'll even make it to the train station before Mother and Dad are back.

After only a few minutes there are at least thirty more people behind her. Lia tries to stay on the outside of the queue, to see what's happening, but the weight of people pushes her inwards, towards the shop's wall.

She holds her bandaged hand in the air, so no one bumps into it by mistake.

There are waves and waves of people, and they keep pushing her into the wall of the grocer's. She tries to see through the shop window, see whether anything is going on inside. *Where is that chicken?*

Lia looks at her watch. It's ten-forty. The way it's looking she probably won't get out of here before Mother and Dad come back.

She makes faces at herself in the shop window.

She tries to push back at the people who are pushing into her. She remembers that the grown-ups like queues. They would probably queue for fun. Just think, how they cheer up when someone tells them about queues. Grown-ups are crazy.

She looks across the narrow street, at the farmers' market

that's been deserted since everyone rushed to the chicken queue. The market is where we should do all our shopping, she thinks. She has told Mother she's happy just eating toast and vegetables. Polenta. There are never queues in the market, well, only that once, for bananas. But Mother had not found out about it in time. Lia had just seen a few of their neighbours returning with these bunches of fat, yellow sickles, and heard the rumour of total mayhem in the queue. That was a legendary queue. She had been very glad to have missed that one, though somehow she got grief anyway: at school the next day she drew a banana and a hammer, and there was no end of trouble. She still shudders at the memory. The banana was exactly like the astronaut: one of those harmless things which change a calm grown-up into a raging maniac. She has never drawn bananas again, and she thinks twice before drawing any other fruit.

'I was here earlier, they held my place!' a woman in a big housecoat in front of Lia is shouting. The woman insists she has the right to rejoin the queue, but she has brought five other friends with her, that's why everyone is angry. Eventually, she gets all five newcomers into the queue.

The time is eleven.

Lia stands up straight, peeks out of the queue. How did this happen? She knows where she was standing compared to the shop entrance, and now, not only has she not moved forward, she has been pushed back. They're cheating. It also looks like the queue is thicker, it's suddenly swollen with people. There must be some eighty people ahead of her.

She has to pay more attention.

Right after this, she gets pinned between the grocer's window and a sticking-out part of the wall. She is stuck there for what seems like forever. The money is wet in her hand and her vest top clings to her back. Chins, breasts and arms hang over her – people have made sunscreens by holding newspapers and bags over their heads. She can't see the sky any more, never mind the street. The thing she can't understand is how, whenever she looks up, the faces around her are new. How are the grown-ups doing it? They sidle up to her, sidle the other way, and suddenly they have sneaked ahead.

It's almost twelve.

Lia pushes and wriggles until she's back on the outside of the queue. She looks down the street. Mother should be here any minute now.

She imagines the bear joining the queue and chasing everyone off. That'll show them! The bear would leave her be, of course. Everyone knows he doesn't harm children. They will split the chicken between them. She will have to explain to him about the frozenness and defrosting. She's sure he doesn't have a freezer in the forest.

Where is Mother, where is Dad? Her watch says it's twelve-fifteen. Lia keeps risking her place in the queue by stepping out and looking down the road for them.

'There you are!' Comrade Popa, Mother's friend and neighbour, comes up to her. 'Your mother called to say your brother ran a sudden fever and they had to go to the doctor. You're not to leave before you have the chicken.'

Before Lia can gather her thoughts to answer, the woman leaves.

It's not possible, Lia wants to shout, they can't do this. It's not fair. She has been here forever, pushed and shoved and stepped on, and they still don't let her go to the station?

She wants to just get out of the queue and run to the station, and then go and live with Comrade Mantea.

She overhears someone near her say, 'Three hundred and fifty? Something like that.' The man is talking about the number of people ahead of them. Three hundred and fifty is a whole mountain of ration cards. The chicken will be finished before she even reaches the door of the grocer's. She's going to end up with no chicken and no parcel.

'Please, will you hold my place for five minutes? I need to pee. I swear I won't bring anyone else with me,' she says this to the kindest-looking neighbour in the queue. She doesn't even have to pretend; she is crying anyway. The old woman nods and she shoots off, as fast as she can, to Comrade Mantea's.

Lia flies up the stairs, four steps at a time.

He is not at home! Lia rings the doorbell and kicks his door, not even caring that neighbours can see or hear. Where is he, today of all days? Unbelievable. He said he would go if she can't.

She slowly heads back for the queue. She is sobbing, and shaking with her whole body. She's afraid to look at her watch. She kicks up the dust and flings the shopping bag at the ground. What a horrible, horrible day. She wipes her face of tears and dust and snot.

Everything went wrong today. She is angry at everyone. At everyone, yes – at Mother, at Dad, at the cheating neighbours in the queue, at Comrade Mantea. How can they ask her to do impossible things? Grown-ups are crazy.

She wipes her face again on her vest top, then hurries back towards the queue. At the corner of the shop complex she turns left instead of right and stops in front of the butcher's. The heavy metal-and-glass doors are padlocked on the inside. She holds the shopping bag and the ration card in her left hand, so everyone on the street can see that she's queuing.

She feels like before a dare, when she doesn't want to do the dare but knows she has no choice.

She just stands in front of the closed doors. Every so often she turns around to see what is happening at the grocer's. The queue is out of sight – it's behind the corner – but by the number of people walking past it she can tell that no one is bothering to join it any more. At some four hundred people it is not worth it; that many chicken claws won't even fit inside the shop.

Lia dares look at her watch. It's 12.47. She watches the little hands move and thinks this must be what it feels like to watch a bomb.

An old man who has been walking down the street with an empty shopping bag stops at the corner of the complex. He puts his hand to his chest and fiddles with the collar of his shirt. He takes a good look at the chicken queue. Lia suspects he's hoping some friend might invite him into the front of the queue. In his left hand his empty canvas shopping bag is twitching. After a minute or so he gives up and continues down the street. Lia turns back to face the butcher's. She can see the man's reflection in the glass door as he walks past her.

Grown-ups love queues, grown-ups love queues, grown-ups love queues.

The old man's head is turned towards Lia and the butcher's.

He has only gone a few paces past her when he stops and says, 'What are you doing, child? Don't you see that the queue is over there? The grocer's door is over there!'

He points at the damned grocer's.

Lia squints up at him, then she turns away. He comes closer. His shopping bag in his trembling hand is twitching again.

'Do you hear me? What are you standing here for?'

She shakes her head.

'What? You can tell me.'

But she can't speak, doesn't know what to say. She tries to make it look like she has a precious secret.

The old man bends down, resting his hands on his thighs. She realises she knows him: he is one of the pensioners who always plays backgammon on a street bench. Pensioners are particularly crazy queuers.

'Child, they're not selling anything here,' the man says. 'The chicken is over there . . .'

He seems less sure.

'Did your parents send you to buy something?'

She nods.

'Chicken?'

She just turns away from him.

'Are you sure?'

She doesn't move a muscle.

He straightens himself up and stands behind her in line. Lia turns and frowns at him.

'What?' he wags a finger at her. 'You're not fooling me!'

The old man then sees an acquaintance pass along the street.

He hollers her over. 'Look, if I let you in on something will you do me a favour and stop by my son's and tell him to just drop everything and come here?' He grabs the woman by the elbow and leans into her. 'Pork,' he says. 'Forget about the chicken claws over there,' pointing his chin at the grocer's.

The woman makes him swear that he will let her into the new queue when she gets back.

Soon about ten grown-ups have taken up positions behind the old man, and every few seconds someone new is joining them. Lia hears them talk of the possibility of veal.

It's 13.19.

She is just counting her queuers again when she sees the housecoat woman who first pushed her back in the chicken queue.

The woman can take the risk of leaving her queue: she probably has a dozen people who owe it to her to hold her place.

'This child,' the housecoat says to another woman. 'She was right next to me in the chicken queue . . . She wouldn't have left a good place for nothing. Oh God!' she wails, and hurries back to her queue.

But of course: the housecoat has packed all her relatives and friends between them, so she has missed the way Lia slipped down in the queue. Lia giggles when she sees the housecoat return with several of her cronies, and take their place at the back of Lia's queue.

The chicken truck finally arrives then, and the unloading starts. Such rotten luck, Lia thinks. If she hadn't been pushed back in the queue, she would have made it.

But in no time, Lia's new queue grows to over one hundred people long. At that point people start leaving the back of the chicken queue in large numbers, thinking they have a better chance in this other line. After they pass the one-hundred-and-fifty mark – it is much easier counting people now that she is at the front – everyone who sees her queue is joining it.

There's a rumour now that even people at the front of the other queue are starting to feel anxious – they are in pole position for chicken but the butcher is bound to have something better. The butcher's! *When was the last time we had something from him?* She realises that the situation will not get better than this. Her stomach begins to hurt. She needs the courage of a master-spy hero for the next step.

A very tall, thin man then approaches them, coming in from the far left like they do in football. He waves his garden-spade hands as if to apologise – *Just a question, folks, just a question!* He crouches in front of Lia.

'Hey, aren't you a clever one?' a woman in the queue shouts.

The man ignores her.

'Look, kid, I'm second in the queue over there,' he points behind them to the grocer's, 'where any moment now they're going to open. They're selling chicken. They're just finishing unloading it. Now, you're first over here.'

He shows her his open hands. Lia holds her breath.

'You see? We could have both the chicken and the veal. You give me your ration card and money, I'll buy you some chicken and then I'll come over here, you let me in, and I'll get some veal. What do you say?'

The old man behind her taps her shoulder.

'Don't be a fool, kid. Veal is worth much more than chicken, ask for something more.'

'Now, we're just helping each other out here, right?' He glares at the old man. 'Nobody wants to be a filthy profiteer, does he?'

She runs as fast as she can, the bag with the frozen wings and claws bumping against her legs. When the tall man came back with her chicken, Lia told the queue that she has to go and put it in the freezer. They said of course, and promised to hold her place.

It's 13.41.

She has never been to the train station by herself, and now that she has to cross half the town to get there she has no good sense of how long it will take. That damned chicken and that damned queue.

She's by the big bridge now. That has to be more than halfway.

She passes the cinema without even stopping to look at the posters, and when she turns the corner she hears a train whistle.

She runs into the train station, goes straight to the fat woman at the ticket office.

'I'm looking . . . for Comrade engineer Rădescu,' she blurts out, trying to catch her breath.

'Line three, all the way back,' the woman says.

Lia runs out of the ticket office and to the crossing. The barrier is down and a train is passing. She hops up and down, waving the train along. 'Go, go! Why are you so slow?'

The last carriage has just passed and she's about to dart off, when she sees a policeman on the other side, right across from her.

He's just standing there.

The barrier lifts. Lia stops in her tracks.

The policeman is looking her way.

She turns away from him. Maybe she can cross way down there, where the policeman can't see her. She takes a few steps back.

Out of the corner of her eye, she sees the policeman is waving. Lia checks both sides and behind her. There's no one else here.

Her teeth are chattering; she realises she's hugging the frozen bag.

She can't believe that a policeman looking at her will not know that she has a secret mission.

If only she had more time. She could go back inside and wait for him to leave. But now, she has to do something, either cross here and walk in front of the policeman, and then back again with the parcel, or to somehow cross between carriages, where there is no real crossing but where the policeman can't see her.

She looks down at the rails. They smell dirty, of pee. Mother always holds her hand when they are at the station, and she says to never cross when the barrier is down, and never to cross anywhere else. But how can she get to the other side then?

When Lia glances back at the policeman she sees he is now crossing over himself. Lia pretends to stare at the sky.

'What's going on, child? Don't tell me you missed your train?'

Why is he talking to her? She can't believe this is happening.

'Hey, you.'

She makes herself look at him. What, what can she say? 'A parcel from my granny,' she blurts out.

'You're waiting for a parcel from your granny? What you got here, then?' The policeman opens her canvas bag and looks inside. He takes out the ration card that's on top of the chicken and checks the stamp.

'Ah, you went shopping today?'

Lia nods.

'Where's that other parcel, then?'

'Line three,' Lia says.

The policeman looks up. He takes her by the hand then and she has no choice; they walk together to the end of line 3.

'Your granny sent a parcel with this train?'

Lia nods.

They stop in front of the high steps into the train engine. The policeman is waiting for her to do something.

Lia leans inside and says out loud, 'Hello! The parcel from my granny?' Shuffling sounds, and then a man pokes his head into the opening. He is smeared in soot and has a soot-covered handkerchief over the lower half of his face. The whites of his eyes are shiny. They grow large like cartoon eyes when he sees the policeman.

'Comrade! Does anyone here have a parcel from this child's grandmother?' the policeman says.

The man looks at Lia, then at the policeman. He goes away for a second and when he returns he gives Lia a small but heavy parcel wrapped in old newspaper. 'JAM' it says on the top.

When Lia looks up again the man has disappeared back into the engine.

'There we go,' the policeman says. 'You'll find your way home?'

Comrade Mantea is delighted when he sees her, pats her head and tells her she is the best collaborator he ever had. 'Not only the smallest one,' he winks at her.

She has also brought the backpack for him to see, much nicer now with several small flags sewn on to the back. He picks it up, looks at it in the weak light of the kitchen bulb. Lia then wants to tell him about her adventure in the queue, about the policeman, but he interrupts her.

'Not bad. Certainly makes you look like an insufferable little patriot.' He opens the backpack and looks inside, then he opens a kitchen drawer and takes out a measuring tape.

'Here, hold it open,' he tells her. He reaches inside and measures the bottom of the backpack.

When he's done he smacks his lips. 'Now go away, I want to get blind drunk.'

'But I have something funny to tell you,' she says.

He raises an eyebrow. She tells him about the queue, how she tricked everyone. She takes extra care over the part with the old man and the twitching bag, how she lured him over. 'See, you can use this trick too, if you're in a really bad queue and you need it,' she says. 'You can have it.'

'Won't you get into trouble, kid?' he finally says. 'I mean, all those people . . . You'll run into them again.'

'But,' she says, 'it's over. And it was funny. And they cheated first.' She doesn't go around being upset at other children when she's lost at a game. It's all fair.

Comrade Mantea is still looking at her thoughtfully. 'If we could all be like you, kid. You see something that is not right, and you just go ahead and try to fix it.'

'Like with the colours,' she says.

'We wouldn't have ended up in this pickle to begin with.'

'I can always feel it in my belly when something isn't fair,' she says. 'Right here,' she points at her navel.

'They will thank us, once they realise what we did. Everyone will wake up.'

'Colours for everyone!' she says.

Comrade Mantea has stopped listening. He's staring into thin air, hugging the backpack to his chest.

11

Snagov, August

A black limousine arrives at the police station, and before Constantin even steps into the car, the small and fastidiously groomed clerk confiscates his gun. In the backseat the clerk also asks for any briefing notes for Ceauşescu, and when Constantin says that he plans to give his notes to the President himself, the man shakes his head and says, 'Not like this.'

He has slept very badly and has that jittery, disoriented feeling that comes with lack of rest. The rules, Constantin keeps telling himself in the car. As long as you remember the rules. Don't die. Don't get arrested.

His stomach is a mess. He's glad he hasn't eaten anything.

It takes half the day to drive to the sprawling presidential summer residence, and once they get there, the limo and clerk vanish into an underground car park and Constantin is left waiting in the blazing August sun outside the palace for at least an hour. 'Shift change,' mutters the harried woman who finally comes to lead him inside. She takes him to a gilded waiting room, and then they forget about him again.

Constantin feels dizzy and nauseous. He keeps touching the sunburnt skin on the bridge of his nose. Could be sunstroke, on top of everything else. He tiptoes over to the door and asks the enormous bodyguard stationed outside for water. Eventually a tray is delivered, with a bottle of ice-cold Borsec that Constantin gulps down in one go.

It's early evening by the time the woman tells him to get ready – the Comrade Leader wants to see him. She also returns his briefing notes. Five pages of normal text have become a whole pile of papers with typed letters at least three centimetres tall.

Constantin looks at the giant typing in disbelief. Maybe sunstroke is, after all, exactly what he needs to get through this.

The old man is having a pedicure and the space in front of him is taken up by an enormous golden bowl, a stool, and two white-coated women kneeling on a rose-coloured, wall-to-wall Persian rug. Two bodyguards stand by the only door out of the opulent room. There's a strong smell of perfume, and under it a faint odour of – what exactly? Constantin can't put his finger on it.

A water stain slowly grows around the foot bowl, turning the rug crimson.

Ceaușescu leans forwards to inspect a toe. 'They hid one from me, didn't they?' he says.

The dictator looks much older and smaller than he appears on TV, with a pale, scrunched-up face and mean pig eyes that remind Constantin of Davidescu. His voice is raspy and weak.

Even as Constantin thinks this, he is genuinely afraid his thoughts might be overheard.

'I'm not sure I understand,' Constantin says. His own voice sounds foreign to him here. He resists an urge to loosen his tie.

'There's no other explanation. When I told them, none of them knew what to say.'

Constantin hopes Ceaușescu will keep speaking until he can catch up with his train of thought.

'One grizzly, or maybe even two, that we didn't get at the time, and then these grizzlies had cubs, and now someone has a secret grizzly colony that they are plotting to use against me. I'm out in the forest hunting all the time, you know. It's dangerous.'

How did I end up here? Constantin thinks. From investigating twenty-three murders, to reassuring Ceaușescu about grizzlies? He retraces the steps in his mind. But there are huge gaps, chasms. *How did I get here?*

He remembers what Titus once said: 'I'm afraid the day will come when we'll all be mad enough to think it's a bear.'

They hear a click-clack then on the marble floor and the Comrade Leader's wife appears in the doorway. Elena walks up to Ceaușescu and starts ranting about a bus stop that some local authority has built, according to her, within spitting distance of one of their summer houses. 'They don't think!' she says.

Another gust of that horrid perfume follows in her wake, but this time Constantin recognises the smell it's trying to hide: old age. They both smell old.

When Elena notices Constantin, she frowns at him. She seems to be searching her memory for some piece of information. He can spot the moment when she finds it. Her face darkens yet more.

'Is this the one who let his own child die?' she says.

Constantin feels the words like a blow. He prepared for many things, but not for this.

Nicolae turns to look at Constantin for the first time. 'The fellow should have been thrown in jail then. We go to great efforts for the country to have more children.'

'It was all in his file,' she says, still glaring at Constantin. 'Most bizarre.'

'Well, he is what they sent us,' Nicolae says. 'Shall we arrest him and have them send another?'

Ceauşescu turns questioningly to the bodyguards.

'It wasn't like that,' Elena says, annoyance in her voice.

Constantin can accept that he must not speak his mind, that he can't risk Tina and Sandu's lives, but how is it possible that he is being held to account by two mass murderers?

'I don't think anyone should have that option in the first place,' he manages to mumble.

The room is too hot. His shirt is sticking to his back. He realises that he actually hates them.

'What's he saying?' Nicolae asks Elena.

'God knows,' Elena shrugs.

'Why don't you just tell someone to call the Town Hall and destroy the bus stop?' Nicolae asks Elena.

'I already did. But I want to know why they don't think for themselves!' She has already turned around and is walking out of the room.

The white-coated women are drying Nicolae's feet with

towels. Abruptly, he turns to the bodyguards and tells them to find the open window and close it, he can feel a draught. 'Nobody thinks for himself,' he echoes his wife's words. One of the men hesitates at first, then leaves his post.

Constantin is acutely aware of this chance to launch himself at Ceaușescu's throat.

'You're here to present the results of your investigation, but all this time you haven't said a word,' Ceaușescu says. 'I don't have more than two feet,' he points at the pedicurists who are finishing applying cream to his feet.

'Apologies. I was waiting to be addressed,' Constantin says. He looks down at the papers with the enormous shouty font, trying to gather his thoughts, which are all over the place. For example: someone, somewhere, is manufacturing vanity typewriters for ancient dictators who refuse to wear glasses.

Why is he putting up with this? Why is anyone?

He starts giving a summary of the case. It is immediately obvious that Ceaușescu likes numbers; whenever one comes up, the old man nods approvingly. Even when Constantin says out loud the total number of victims, something about Ceaușescu's reaction tells him that he likes the fact that it's a big number, and would find it yet more impressive the bigger it was.

Then, the click-clack again. 'But wait a minute – what's the fellow actually saying?' she shouts from the door already. 'What are we to do about this beast?'

'I am planning it right now, dear, I was just taking in all the facts.'

'Planning it right now? What have the police been doing

all this time? They were supposed to come up with solutions. Make it stop.'

'I have a suspect,' Constantin says. This makes both of them turn to him. They look astonished.

'We have a suspect,' Elena repeats.

'You found my grizzlies?' Nicolae asks.

The second bodyguard returns.

Constantin explains to them about the loner who was living in the Western Carpathians, was seen in the company of bears, and who first started living as a hermit after being released from prison after serving a five-year sentence for sedition. The details were vague but Constantin gathered the man had protested at the bread ration being halved. Constantin wants to show them a photo of the man, but when he stands up from his chair both bodyguards leap at him. In the end he gives the photo to the guard, who hands it over to the couple. The picture shows a wild face; a bushy white beard and hateful stare.

The hermit is as innocent of these crimes as can be, but he is also already dead and has no known relatives that can be harassed. Constantin found him in a morgue, dead from exposure, and he removed his ID and replaced the death certificate. It will take a while before any investigator can rule him out as a suspect. The hermit has to buy him some time until he has made some real progress on the case.

'Now, we just have to find this man,' Constantin says.

Nicolae is still staring at the photo. Elena is pacing the room, her head down, concentrating.

'The file,' she finally says, and holds out her hand to

Constantin. He gives her the papers. She leaves the room with them.

'I don't remember this face,' Nicolae says thoughtfully, and reclines back in the armchair.

'A state has many enemies,' Constantin says. 'No man can know them all.'

'I was sure it would be one of the gamekeepers,' Nicolae says. 'Though it's true we have questioned them all. They swore they hadn't pilfered any grizzlies.'

'But the gamekeepers have access to guns, correct?' Constantin says, trying to inject some sanity into the conversation. 'Wouldn't that be . . . easier than training a bear to kill? I don't think we're looking for a gamekeeper.'

Ceaușescu turns to him, and for a moment those small eyes seem vicious and cunning rather than old. 'Oh, but they don't dare do it directly like that,' Ceaușescu says. 'Nobody in the whole world dares.'

There are three paces between him and the old man, and about six between the bodyguards and Ceaușescu. What can he achieve in half a second?

He answers his own question: he can remember Sandu and Tina.

They hear the heels again then, and Elena comes back in. She throws the folder in his lap.

'Well, this is useless,' she says. 'Not a word about why the beast is following us.'

'Following you?' Constantin says.

Elena turns to Nicolae, makes a despondent gesture. 'Here we are. Explaining the case to our own police.'

'To be fair to them,' Ceauşescu says, 'that's why we stopped having the bear on the news. So no one would catch on and embarrass us. It worked.'

Constantin is lost in incomprehension. Elena goes up to the bodyguard who had left the room earlier and tells him something, after which the man leaves again.

The bodyguard returns with a map. Constantin unfolds the map but is none the wiser. It looks like the 'TV map' – the one the investigation shares with the TV news. There are red crosses that coincide with the location of the murders, and short date intervals next to each one. Yes, it's a map of the attacks, and the intervals overlap with the dates of the killings. There's only one red cross on the map that does not have a date interval next to it.

Elena jabs a finger at it. 'It's a dated map of my husband's trips. You will notice the extremely significant overlap with the location of the attacks.'

'Yes,' Ceauşescu says. 'All except one murder are within fifteen kilometres of the town I was visiting at the time.'

Is this true? They are obviously insane, but this bit: could it be true? The places and dates coincide. The killer must be someone who travels with Ceauşescu, and has access to the Securitate archives. Constantin's mind races. Then: we could have given out warnings. Relevant warnings, if these two ghouls had just told us where they would be. So many deaths could have been avoided.

Elena says, 'So. Why are we briefing you about the investigation, and not the other way around?'

Because I had no reason to ask for your whereabouts,

Constantin thinks. Because twenty million people zone out whenever they show your faces on the news, so we wouldn't have noticed where you are anyway. Because the whole state apparatus would have wanted to ignore this aspect, had I noticed and told anyone.

'Can I keep this?' Constantin asks.

'Not so crazy now, is it?' Ceauşescu smiles at him with his little pig eyes. 'My grizzly theory.'

'The killer is someone who travels with you,' Constantin says. 'I need to speak to everyone in your entourage. To the person who organises your trips and knows who travels with you. Now, tonight.'

He needs the list of everyone who has travelled with Ceauşescu on each occasion. Which ones are also Securitate agents. Their age, their physical condition. That map! He's looking at it and he can still hardly believe it. The solution to the murders was broadcast weekly on the news; everyone just needed to put two and two together. Each new cross that appeared on the bear map was in or near the town that was on the news at around the same time because Ceauşescu had been visiting there. There would have been a couple of days' difference in the announcements, and sometimes the killings and the state visits were in slightly different towns, but still: the news, truthful and useful for once. And he had missed every clue.

'But why would the killer attack other people if he's already in our entourage?' Nicolae asks, looking confused.

'And with a bear, too,' Elena says.

Constantin no longer knows how to reply to this nonsense.

'Someone who is travelling with you has killed twenty-three people,' he helplessly repeats.

'No. Someone is following us,' Ceaușescu said, his voice menacing.

He tries some more, but it's impossible to convince them that they're not the ones in danger.

They get rid of him after that; a giant of a bodyguard comes to escort him out. Constantin, drained after the meeting, just lets things happen to him. His thoughts drift. He feels processed, dealt with.

He follows the bodyguard through long corridors and grand halls. He feels numb. The killer is most likely here in the palace. The thick carpeting dampens the sound of their footsteps. He sees newsreels before his eyes, Ceaușescu and Elena waving at adoring crowds in some provincial town. He should have paid attention. If he stays close to the bodyguard, he can't see where he's heading for the man's enormous back. Opulence flashes by on either side. Leather-padded doors soft-close behind him. He felt hungry at some point today, but that's gone now. The killer is here, but they're getting rid of the detective.

Constantin is not entirely sure he's still himself. There's a real detective somewhere who would get his green ink pen and scribble on the gilded walls.

They step outside. It's dusk already. Gravel crunches under-foot; he finds it comforting. He loosens his tie and looks around in the weak light, expects to see the limo that brought him here. He'll have a nap in the car on the way home. It will do him good. But no, there's no car. It looks like the man intends to simply dump him outside the palace gates. Constantin fills his lungs: it smells of linden and distant summer fires.

Does all gravel make this sound, this satisfying crunch, or is there special palace gravel? He stops; looks down. He lifts one foot, then the other.

Constantin smiles to himself: *Daddy! The story*, Sandu would say, hauling him out of fog and daydreams.

It's thirty kilometres to the nearest town. He's in the middle of a forest. It's almost night. Suddenly Constantin feels like he's surfacing, gasping for air. If the killer didn't suspect the investigation was on to him before this, he'll be certain now.

'My service weapon,' Constantin says, stopping in his tracks just inside the gate. 'I need it back.'

He made it out of that room with the two lunatics. He has to make it all the way home.

'Nobody said nothing about that,' the bodyguard says. He grabs Constantin by the arm.

'It's state property.' Constantin, feeling like a recalcitrant mutt next to the giant, resists being pulled along. 'I'm a police inspector, I'm not legally allowed to leave it behind.' With his free hand Constantin searches inside his pocket and produces his police ID.

The bodyguard squints at it in the dark. He hesitates. Clearly, nobody informed him Constantin is police.

Finally the man relents, leaves Constantin in the care of the soldiers manning the gate, and heads back to the palace.

Constantin is alert now. He tries to remember the way he came here. It was a few hundred metres of country road through dense forest, then the motorway. Once he gets to the motorway he'll be fine; he'll just wave his gun and stop a car.

He takes a sideways glance at the young soldiers. They seem uninterested in him.

They all hear footsteps then, and turn to see the bodyguard. The man puts the gun in Constantin's hand.

'Open up,' the bodyguard tells the soldiers.

Constantin can feel the gun is too light. He should protest. But the bodyguard places a hand on his shoulder, turns him around and gives him a shove.

The gates shut behind Constantin.

A moment's hesitation, then he slinks off the road and into the forest. He hides behind a tree. Hoping against hope, he checks the gun. It's empty.

His knees, his damn knees are shaking. He hasn't felt this kind of fear before. He waits for it to pass, thinks it's a wave, but no. It's here to stay.

He takes a moment to clear his thoughts. He reckons he'll be most vulnerable once he's a bit away from the palace; the killer will not want any screams to be heard inside. Would the bear use a gun in this situation, or would he stick to his signature cutting tools?

'Come and stab me, you bastard,' Constantin mutters. 'Don't ruin your reputation.'

Images of the slashed bodies that are the bear's signature flash before his eyes. Constantin suddenly feels soft, aware he's all exposed soft tissue. Something horribly like a whimper escapes him.

He starts running in the shallow ditch by the side of the road.

Another unwelcome vision: Vasile, a few days from now, poring over photographs of Constantin's hacked body.

He tries to jump over the tangle of shoots but half the time he's crawling: he stumbles on brambles and falls over, thorns tearing through his trousers. It's really too dark to run. Each time he's flat on the ground his spine tingles, and something like a vice at the back of his neck tightens as he waits for a blow. When it doesn't come, he gets up, keeps running. His mind, meanwhile, latches on to an absurd idea: he never snitched for the Securitate. Maybe the bear won't even bother with him.

He notices something further ahead. He slows down. He can only see an outline on the side of the road. It could be a parked van, or truck. It's large.

He stops, panting, tries to get a better look at whatever is ahead. He can't see, damn it. Can't see what it is and if it's empty. He considers going deeper into the forest to go round and past the vehicle.

He hears a car engine then. But it's coming from behind, from the palace. Constantin takes a few steps into the forest and hides behind a tree.

The car is approaching very slowly.

Constantin falls on all fours and searches the ground for something to defend himself with, should it come to that. But it's just bits of rotting wood, thin rods. He can't even find a rock.

He has an idea. He takes off his belt and loops it through the gun trigger, makes a knot. He's made himself a kind of flail. Gives him maybe a metre's reach.

He can see the lights of the car now. No – it's a flashlight.

The driver is scanning the side of the road. Constantin knows he should run further into the forest, but he can't bring himself to do it. It would mark the actual start of a hunt.

He makes himself as small as possible behind the trees and bushes.

The car is level with him now. It's barely inching along. The beam of the flashlight zigzags around Constantin.

The car passes. Constantin is still holding his breath.

And then it stops. The engine dies. Constantin sees the flashlight returning. It's searching the place where he veered into the forest. Where the roadside brambles no longer appear trampled.

Constantin swears under his breath. He grasps the belt with both hands.

The car door opens. One person steps out. The door closes.

Then, nothing. The man must be listening. Constantin's own heartbeat sounds hopelessly loud.

And then, out of nowhere, another engine. Noisy, rumbling. The van or truck that was parked further down the road has come to life.

It sounds like some kind of road maintenance vehicle, like it's scraping the ground. It makes a hellish racket. Constantin is anxious that he can no longer hear the first driver's steps.

The vehicle stops in front of the car.

'You're going to have to move that for us,' someone shouts down from the cab.

Constantin risks turning to look at the road, but he can only see the large vehicle's blinding headlights.

Nothing happens for a long moment. Then, footsteps. The

car door opens and closes. The engine starts. The car reverses a few metres, then it does a sharp U-turn and heads back towards the palace.

Constantin closes his eyes and breathes out. Gives a heartfelt thanks to any and all gods he doesn't believe in. He feels weak; for a moment he's little more than a human-shaped puddle of relief.

He gathers himself and stands up, steps out of the forest. Raises his hands and holds the police ID high in his right hand. They'll take him for a madman with his torn clothes; a wild apparition.

He walks towards the headlights. He still can't see a thing.

Getting closer, he makes out the shape of some kind of tractor-digger.

'Hello, Comrade! Police officer here.'

Nothing.

Constantin stops. A thought comes to him that instantly makes him feel ill. But it's not possible. He's not Vasile, he won't have misjudged a situation so badly. 'Hello?' he tries again. He's poised to turn and run back into the forest. 'I'm a police officer. I need a lift.'

'You need some fucking bear spray is what you need.'

The shiny bald head that sticks out of the tractor's cab belongs to Titus. The voice belongs to Titus. It still takes Constantin a few seconds to understand that the whole blessed man is Titus.

'You! What are you doing here?'

He hops into the cab. They hug. Constantin rests his head on the dashboard for a moment. He must be the luckiest man alive.

'Let's put some road between us and this lot,' Titus says and turns the tractor around.

'Did you get a look at him?' Constantin asks.

'That was our killer?'

'I'll explain, you won't believe it,' Constantin says. 'Did you see him?'

Titus shakes his head. 'Collar pulled up, cap.'

'Tall? Short? Fat? Bear?'

'It's not enough I saved your ass?'

'God, yes! You're alone?'

'Yeah. I said "us" to make him think there's a whole tractor cavalry round the corner.' Titus gives Constantin a big smile.

'But how come you're here? And what's with the tractor?'

'I got antsy. Thought you would get in trouble, one way or another.'

They're at the junction with the motorway. One step closer to home.

'I came with my car,' Titus says, 'thought I'd wait here, but they patrol this stretch of road, they're not letting anyone just dick around. So I found a farmhouse and gave the guy some cigarettes, left my car as guarantee. The palace patrols let me drive up and down here as long as I'm pretending to clear the side of the road. It's actually pretty fucking relaxing, I'll show you.'

Constantin is so grateful he's in danger of being sentimental. 'Titus. Anyone who doesn't know better would say you're an intelligent man.'

12

Sighişoara and Piteşti, August

'Our grand rehearsal!' Comrade Mantea announces. 'Finally.'

It is the afternoon before the Dear Leader meeting. They are in the kitchen. Comrade Mantea looks very different from bathrobe-and-matchstick old man. His beard is gone, he's had a haircut, and his hair is combed back instead of looking ruffled and spiky. He has put something shiny in his hair, too, and if Lia could reach all the way up she would be very tempted to touch it. He even smells nice. Come to think of it – Lia looks around – the flat itself is clean and tidy. For once.

'You look very nice,' Lia says. 'You could be on TV.'

He gives her a funny look. 'We need to be prepared for all eventualities,' he says.

A light brown suit hangs from the curtain railing, a fat tie across one shoulder. He tells her that's his National Day Parade outfit. Lia notices a shiny gold pin on the lapel, and when she looks closer she sees it's a small crown. 'What's that?' she asks.

'Oh, I just wanted to mark the occasion somehow. I'm not a damn royalist either; they can all put their sceptres and swastikas and sickles where the sun doesn't shine. But that's the closest thing I could find to an anti-government, pro-colour symbol.' He winks at her.

'Mother is going to braid my hair,' Lia says. 'They made me cut my toenails.'

Comrade Mantea suddenly takes her face in his hands and kisses the top of her head. 'Can you believe it's happening? Here, have a seat' – he pulls out a chair – 'and let's go through the last details.'

He repeats the things they have already discussed. She will take the Dear Leader's present now, and in the morning, after Mother packs her lunch in the backpack, she will go to the bathroom, empty the lunchbox, and put the present under the false bottom that Comrade Mantea has made in the backpack. The food she has to hide somewhere in the bathroom until she can get rid of it properly.

'You need to empty the lunchbox for the weight, yes? If someone wonders why the backpack is so heavy, you just show them the lunchbox.'

'I put a hammer and sickle on the backpack!' she says. She shows him the bag, full of little flags made out of coloured fabric, and the paper hammer and sickle that she cut out from a schoolbook and glued to the backpack.

'Lia, look at me.' Comrade Mantea is very serious. 'You won't open the present before you give it to Comrade Ceaușescu, yes? Don't look at me like that, I know you! You're more curious than a tree-full of fabulously curious monkeys. You can't help yourself, you'll want to check, but believe me you'll ruin it. All our work will have been for nothing. No more colours, no more anything.'

She nods. 'And I can only speak to Comrade Ceaușescu about the colours after he sees the present.'

'Correct.'

'But then, I can tell him everything, about the colours they have in Germany, about our Christmas tree, how there's never anything with colour to buy. I know he likes colour, too, or else he wouldn't come just for the National Day Parade. Maybe there are people who are keeping all this a secret from him. Maybe he doesn't know.'

This would be the easiest solution. If the Dear Leader doesn't even know about the missing colours, then he will be very angry with the people who are not giving us more of them. He will be grateful she has told him. If, on the other hand, he already knows about it, then there must be some other reason for this miserable state of things. He will have to be persuaded that it is wrong.

'I hope it's a very good present,' she says to Comrade Mantea.

'The absolute best, you can bet your nose on that. I've been thinking, and the ideal moment to give it to him is when you are in the open-top car together. From the Town Hall to the Pioneers' Park it will just be the two of you and the driver, so no one can interfere and take the present from you. That car ride will also give you the chance to tell him about the colours.'

'Where will you be?'

'I'll be in the crowd, as close to you as I can possibly get.'

*   *   *

At home that evening, Mother and Dad are going over the next day's schedule. They are excited, too, but in a nervous way. Mother sits Lia in an armchair and plonks Dani on the sofa next to her. 'I need everyone to be still so I can get my thoughts in order.'

She and Dad will also go to the Parade, as special guests of the Mayor. Mother has been to the hairdresser. Dad has learned everything about his factory's targets. Mother used half their flour ration to make a big batch of biscuits that she hopes will keep Dani quiet tomorrow. Dad has polished his good shoes. Right now, Mother is running around and preparing everyone's clothes.

'This needs ironing. This, too. This . . . damned moths!'

Dad is leaning against the doorframe, stroking his chin. 'It's not too late, you know. We could give her something tomorrow that will make her too sick to take part.'

'What?' Lia says. 'After all the special classes?'

Mother keeps looking at the pale blue dress that she is holding up.

'Don't tell me you wouldn't be relieved,' Dad says to Mother, ignoring Lia. 'I know I'll sleep a whole lot better tonight.'

'One hundred days of special classes!' Lia shouts.

'The teacher will understand. She'll probably thank us,' Dad says.

'I thought you were dying to get out of this,' Mother turns to her.

'Not any more. I learned so much.'

Mother and Dad exchange a look.

'I'm not eating anything, not one thing, until after the Parade,' Lia announces. 'I'm not hungry.'

Dad covers his eyes with his hand and shakes his head.

'This kid . . .'

'I can eat her food,' Dani says.

Mother turns back to the wardrobe. 'Victor, to be honest I think it's a bit late for second thoughts. We just have to pray to our lucky stars.'

Dad comes and sits next to her on the sofa.

'Lia. Look at me. I know things are difficult and complicated. A lot of the time we're not making sense. One day, when you are old enough, you'll understand, and you'll realise we did our best. But you have to just believe us now. It's very important that you behave tomorrow. You don't want anything bad to happen to us, do you?'

She has heard speeches like this before. She doesn't believe it: people are talking about terrible things happening, they hint in a sneaky way that they have happened, but at the same time everyone pretends they don't happen. How bad can they truly be, these bad things that everyone can pretend didn't happen?

'It's not a joke. If you don't do exactly as you are told tomorrow, Mother and Dad will go to prison. You and Dani will have to go to an orphanage, where they will shave your heads and feed you leftovers.'

Dad is looking at Lia as though she has done something bad. She doesn't know what to say.

'I don't want to frighten you,' Dad says, 'but at the same time I really need you to understand how serious this is.'

'We had a lot of encouraging signs lately, Victor,' Mother says. 'She's spent so much time on that damn backpack. I thought she would be bored of it, but no, after we went to the trouble of sewing on the flags, she also wanted the hammer and sickle.' Mother strokes Lia's head. 'Really, there's been a change. We have to trust that it's enough.'

'I've been thinking,' Dad says, 'if it all goes well, we'll apply to buy that bicycle. There's still going to be a waiting list, they're not making that many of them, but hopefully we can get one before the end of the year.'

'The Pegasus?'

'It might even help with that waiting list that you have met the Dear Leader and made our town proud,' Mother says.

'All right, but I'm still not eating anything,' Lia says.

'Yes, well,' Titus says.

They are in his university office, but Titus is sitting in a low canvas lounger, his feet up on a stool. He has just explained to Constantin that the other day he had 'some kind of chest thing'.

'You're a doctor,' Constantin says, 'you can't talk like that. *Some kind of chest thing?*'

Titus waves at the pack of cigarettes on his desk. 'It's these bastards.'

'Are you OK now?'

Titus nods. 'De-tarring my lungs as we speak. So. The archives.' He points towards the cassette player. Constantin presses 'play' and braces himself for the first ominous notes.

In the last two days, Constantin and Titus have travelled separately to two towns each where bear murders have taken place. Constantin asked Titus to go instead of sending Vasile because it's such a delicate task; it takes someone intelligent to tease out information from Securitate staff. So, the coroner left his university basement and spent precious petrol on the trip, but the agents there didn't even consider letting him speak to the archivists. They almost had him arrested. 'Look, if you want anything like this done,' Titus said over the phone, 'you've got to send your assistant. At least he's a policeman. They don't tolerate the likes of me snooping around there.'

Titus's voice had suddenly sounded old and tired. And then, the *chest thing*. He takes in Titus's outstretched body. 'You're sure you're up for this?'

'Spiffing. This' – Titus pats the side of the lounger – 'it's just to make it more difficult for me to get up and grab a cigarette. Go on.'

Constantin wasn't much luckier in his towns. He showed up with his police badge and official request with the Minister of the Interior's stamp, and yes, he was granted access to the relevant part of the archives, but the archivists he tried to question about who had accessed the files looked at him as though he were mad. Common mortals may be cowed enough to snitch on their fellow citizens, but Securitate staff clearly aren't.

'So. We're looking for a fit male who travels with Ceauşescu and who is a Securitate agent. The normal thing to do would be to obtain a shortlist of suspects from the presidential administration. As we know, they're unwilling to provide that. So, we've got to narrow it down from hundreds of people. Doctors, cooks, security, servants, drivers, advisors, senior Party people and their security, their children and their tutors and trainers . . . And many others who follow the President around without actually travelling with him, such as a TV, radio and press team. That alone is about forty people. It'll take ages to interrogate everybody, even if they let us.'

'Bottom line,' Titus says, 'there's a lot riding on those archives of yours.'

'Look, we just need one out of some two dozen archivists to remember an unexpected visit,' Constantin says.

'Wrong. We also need them to be willing to share this particular memory with us.'

'Yes. But we hold a trump card. That one town where the bear claimed a victim, but which Ceauşescu wasn't visiting at the time.'

'Could the murder have been misattributed?' Titus asks.

Constantin wonders if Titus is taking some memory-impairing medication.

'I know, I know. It was me who confirmed it was the bear.'

'Plus, it happened before anyone knew this was a serial killer, and the facts of the case matched the pattern that was only revealed afterwards. It was the bear.'

'You think he lives there?' Titus asks.

'I don't see how he could live up there and still be working for the presidential administration. More likely that he had some other reason to visit. Maybe he's from there.'

'You want to try those particular archives, then.'

'But not only because of that. Ceauşescu happens to be going there in three days. For the National Day celebrations. With any luck . . .'

Titus taps the side of his nose. 'Aha. That particular Securitate archivist will have seen our bear twice.'

'It's a good chance.'

'You don't look too excited,' Titus says. 'Actually, you look worse than me. What's going on?'

Constantin has hardly slept since the palace visit. The first night he kept waking up, expecting to see the killer loom over him. He realised he was risking Sandu and Tina's lives by staying there, so the next day he moved into a hotel, told Tina and Sandu he was on a stakeout. Anyone wants to kill him, at least his family is not in the way.

But he still can't sleep.

Constantin, in a hurry, opens the door to his hotel room. He looks at his watch; it's not too late. He loosens his tie and sits down on the bed. Puts the telephone on his knee.

'Daddy! It's story time.'

'Hello to you, too.'

Constantin tries to sound cheerful.

'I didn't forget,' Sandu says.

'Of course you didn't. Are you comfortable? Where are you?'

'In the hallway by the phone.'

'I see. Well, take it to the armchair in the living room. You can unspool the cord, it's long.'

He waits for Sandu to move the phone.

'I'm ready!' Sandu says.

Constantin opens the green ink book. This one is a story he doesn't really want to tell, or not yet, but he needs Sandu to know, in case something happens to him. The boy has to learn to fear lies, to understand that they can become truth in the worst way possible.

'Once upon a time there was a land so far, far away that you had to travel many times around the world before you landed on its shores. In this land darkness always reigned. The people of this land had never seen the sun, or the moon, or even the light given by fire. They went to church in the dark, they worked the land in the dark, they ate in the dark. They defended themselves against the hungry bears that roamed the forests around their village in the dark. It sounds terrible, doesn't it?'

'I've closed my eyes, Daddy.'

'Very good, that's what it was like. But these people, driven by their sightless necessity, had discovered a different kind of light. They all had a torch made from the wood of a mysterious tree that only grew at the bottom of an enchanted valley, and which burned with a flame that cast something that was not light, but truth. You could shine the torch in a stall-holder's face at the market, and you would immediately know if he was trying to pull one over on you, or you could shine the torch at a clump of trees and you would know if bears lurked behind them. And, because it was so easy to test if someone was a friend or foe, if they were telling the truth or not, the people of this land were actually by and large honest, and crimes were so rare that the people needed their torch only for the most trivial things, such as to see when a child is lying about being hungry because he just wants to keep playing, or if a watermelon is ripe. See, it wasn't that terrible after all.'

Sandu doesn't say anything; Constantin can feel him pondering whether it was worth giving up sight for this mysterious truth-torch.

'Well, in this land there was a little boy who had lost his parents to sickness, and now lived alone with a donkey and what help he received from the other villagers. To this little boy, the torch was more valuable than anything, because he didn't have the wisdom of his parents to help guide him, and no wealth of past experiences. The others, they often put their torches down – when together with their families, or with friends – and they thought the little boy with his always lit torch and his donkey was a bit of a dullard and an annoyance.

'Maybe, even, the villagers had become so accustomed to rarely having to face the torch, that they did try to pull a fast one now and again, and they were embarrassed when this innocent boy came along with his donkey and shone the torch in their faces, showing them to have not been entirely honest.

'Now, the original details are lost in the fog of history, but we know that some villagers began making rules about when the torch should be used. They advised people to refrain from using the torch at the market, or when lovers had been apart for a longer time. "No one is saying to cross the bear-infested woods without a torch, God forbid, but surely we don't need the damn thing in our houses, among family and friends?" Some villagers, trying to lead by example, started leaving their houses without their torch altogether, just to show their blind faith in their fellow citizens.

'The boy, who didn't have anyone to take care of him or to reassure him about the world and its intentions, was very loath to abandon the torch, and tried to sneak it with him whenever possible, hiding it in the donkey's mane or in the bread basket.

'Now, of course, there were other villagers besides our boy

who were not entirely happy with these new rules. Women, for instance, who relied on the torch when out and about in case some evildoer was lying in wait for them, they felt vulnerable at having to go and fetch water in the total dark. But the village elders told them that their neighbours found their behaviour insulting, and who, pray, would be such a monster as to attack an innocent woman? The village elders made them realise that they had only been thinking of their own feelings. Many still didn't agree, but they thought it safer to just stay at home than to go against the village elders. Soon, the streets at night had only men.

'A similar thing happened to our boy. He got his ears cuffed whenever neighbours saw him out with his torch, so he went out less and less, or only when he thought no one else would be around. He sat in his little hut, hugging the torch. *If only I could talk to Mother and Father*, the boy thought, *they would tell me what to do.*

'Little by little things started happening in the village: money disappeared from someone's purse, the wine was watered down in the village pub. A string of cellar burglaries. But all this was talked about in hushed voices because no one dared speak in favour of using the torches. And one man, who was the main suspect for several of the misdeeds, he stood up in the village square and smashed his torch to bits with a hammer. He was named a hero and inspiration to all those who were still weakly clinging to their torches.

'Our boy kept himself to himself, tried to feed his donkey with grass from around his hut and to live off the potatoes and cabbages that grew in his garden. He lost touch with what was happening in the village. And in the end, the poor orphan boy decided that this was no way to live, alone and frightened, and so one morning he packed his few belongings, fed the donkey, and set off into the world in search of a more friendly home. But he wanted to have one last proper look at the village where he had been born, and where his parents had lived, and so he shone his torch over the village. And what do you think he saw? The village streets were full of hungry bears.'

Constantin's free hand is closed into a fist: he knows Sandu would have been holding his hand by now if they had been sitting together.

'The boy finds a better village?' Sandu asks.

Constantin is aching to hug him.

'It will not be easy.' His voice trembles. 'But the boy knows that he has his entire life before him and must keep looking for a better place.'

Constantin lets him go then, tells him goodnight. He hopes he hasn't given him nightmares. Such a good boy. Too good for the bears.

Lia is standing on the steps of the Town Hall. It's sunny and very hot. For as far as she can see, the main street is lined with bunting. People wave little flags, waiting for the Dear Leader and his wife to arrive and the parade to start. The whole town looks like it has received a good scrubbing – the streets are clean and even the windows of the road-facing houses have been washed. Potholes are gone. It's as though the town and its houses were just taken new and shiny out of a box.

She has been squinting at the bright light for some time

now but hasn't spotted Comrade Mantea in the crowd. It's difficult, with so many people there and all the men wearing suits. Mother, Dad and Dani are inside the main room of the Town Hall, together with other important people. She saw Comrade Mantea's son in the Town Hall, too, talking to the Mayor; at first she was afraid that he would recognise her, but then she remembered she had been hiding in Comrade Mantea's bedroom when he visited.

Outside here it's just Lia in her parade uniform, some pioneer flag-bearers either side of the wide steps, and various people rushing up and down. At one point, she spots the open-top car that's supposed to take her and the Dear Leader across town driving past the Town Hall and into a gated car park.

Everyone is keeping an eye on the sky in the direction of the football field. People are saying the Dear Leader will come in his own helicopter, and land there. So far there's only a tricolour kite in the sky.

Along the main road there's balloons, big flags flying from lamp posts, and freshly planted flowers in the red, blue and yellow of the flag. So much colour. And there's still the military parade to come – they'll bring big brass instruments that shine like gold treasures in the sun. If she didn't have an important mission she'd be completely beside herself, as the grown-ups say. Lia imagines wandering the streets with a second Lia next to her, and twice the colour excitement.

From afar, she can vaguely hear a loudspeaker and words that sound like the kind of poem that she'll have to recite.

Lia shades her eyes again and searches the crowd for Comrade Mantea. Then, for the millionth time this morning, she reaches behind her and pats the backpack. She had no trouble this morning: the packed lunch is at the back of the bathroom cupboard, the present is under the false bottom, and the empty lunchbox on top of it. No one has asked to see inside the backpack, and no one questioned her bringing it to the meeting. She was so nervous at breakfast that she needed to go to the toilet three times. Mother and Dad almost had their way – her stuck in the toilet and missing the Dear Leader.

A whole hour passes like this. Nothing happens, nobody comes. She is in the shade now, luckily the Town Hall is blocking the sun, but it's still very hot. Her feet are beginning to hurt.

Now and then when someone comes running up or down the steps, she calls out to ask them about when the Dear Leader is coming, but they don't stop to talk to her. The people lining the street have grown tired, too. There's a lot less waving. She can no longer hear any poems or music from the Pioneers' Park.

She wonders if she will hear or see the helicopter first.

When she turns around yet again to see if anyone is coming, Comrade Mantea's son is just stepping out of the Town Hall, lighting a cigarette. He winks at her. She gives him her most evil look, and turns away again. She makes an effort to stand up straight.

She hears steps behind her.

'Everyone is upset that Comrade Ceauşescu isn't here yet, but I think you're the most upset of them all.'

She will not speak to him to punish him for being mean

to Comrade Mantea. She clasps the backpack straps with her hands.

'That's a very pretty backpack,' he nudges her. 'As soon as I noticed it I said to myself, now that's a very dedicated little pioneer.'

She looks around. Everyone is still in the Town Hall. The people are still lining the road. The open-top car is still in the car park.

Comrade Mantea's son sits down on a step and pats the spot next to her. He puffs on his cigarette.

He can't be so bad if he can appreciate the colours on her backpack. Lia sits down, too, a bit further away.

'We are supposed to go in the car together,' she says. 'Why is he so late? I went to special classes. The whole summer.'

Comrade Mantea's son shrugs. 'Know what? Maybe it's about the bear. Lots of plans have been changed because of the bear.'

'Comrade Mantea was sure they hadn't caught it,' she says, and only realises her mistake after the words have come out. He turns to her. 'Comrade Mantea?'

Constantin holds up the document as though it's a cross and he's exorcising demons. It's the paper authorising the police to access the Securitate archives with the lowest secrecy classification, and it has worked so far on the door guard at the innocuous-looking Securitate office building, then on their front desk, and now he is testing the document's powers one floor up, on Comrade archivist Veta, a rosy-cheeked woman in her sixties with a fiery chestnut perm.

The woman takes the paper from him and puts on her glasses. Intentionally, he's sure, she's blocking his path to the archive room behind her. But he does not really care about the archives.

'It is of the utmost importance that I consult some documents in your archive,' Constantin says while she's reading. He pretends he's trying to look over her into the room. 'You'll see it has the Minister's signature,' he taps the document.

It's early in the morning but it's gearing up to be an extremely hot day, and all the windows are open. In the room behind Comrade Veta, Constantin catches sight of papers flying off a desk.

Comrade Veta looks up at him. 'Today, you come? The one day this decade the Comrade President is visiting us? You're lucky I'm not at home, getting ready for the parade.'

Constantin nods. 'You're very welcome to leave, I can study the archive on my own.' He sighs. 'Unfortunately this matter is important enough for a police officer to miss the festivities.'

'Ha! That's not what this document says,' Comrade Veta waves the paper at him. 'We're supposed to grant access to a small part of the archives. There's no talk of anyone being left alone in there.'

She turns her back to him and enters the archive room. Constantin follows her. 'You can have a look at everything in section 2B of the archive,' she says. 'With me right here.'

He knows the type: anything he asks for she will refuse if she can. Out of habit, out of perverse impulse. Comrade Veta has no choice but to let him look at those particular files, but if he had said he's really there to question her, she would have let him make paper planes out of any files. And not spoken to him at all.

A few minutes later, Constantin has collected a sizeable stack of files and sits down at the desk to 'study' them. Comrade Veta has followed him around the room, making sure that he only opens drawers with the '2B' classification, and painstakingly noting every file he removes.

'Seems quiet here today,' Constantin says after a while. 'I'm guessing all the agents are providing security for the President.'

She looks at him over her glasses; he can see her pondering if she should deign to answer him. 'Security is the result of year-round efforts,' she finally says. 'It's not something provided overnight.'

'Of course,' Constantin says. 'Anyhow, I'm sure the President travels with his own security contingent.'

Did she just scoff at that? It was barely audible, but he could swear Comrade Veta just scoffed.

'You don't think the President has sufficient protection?' he asks.

'Bucharestians,' she shrugs. 'If you want a job done, would they be your first choice?'

It's Constantin's turn to shrug. 'I wouldn't know. I'm never there.'

The woman now gives him a look as though he has just confessed his utter insignificance in the greater scheme of things.

Constantin laughs. 'To be honest, I only got this bear case because nobody else wanted the trouble.'

Comrade Veta nods. 'Anyone sane wouldn't have touched that case with a bargepole.'

The conversation stalls, and they have strayed from the subject of the President's visit. Constantin allows some time to pass before he dares speak again.

'Are you from here?' he asks.

'Born and raised,' she says.

'Children?'

'Twin boys. Your age.'

'May they live long,' Constantin says. 'I have a son, too.'

She doesn't reply, and Constantin returns to his files. He still feels bad for frightening Sandu with that fairy tale. Tina was furious with him, almost to the point of speaking to him. *The poor boy woke up howling!*

He looks at his watch. Ninety minutes have passed, he's halfway through his stack. He's beginning to panic. What's the magic question?

He turns to look through the window. 'I should probably just give it a break today and enjoy the festivities.'

The woman points at his dwindling stack, 'Come on, you're almost done. I don't want you back here.'

'Was I that much trouble?' Constantin asks. Tries to sound hurt.

She shrugs.

'You often get agents from Bucharest bothering you for stuff?'

Constantin is not even raising his eyes to look at her. He's fascinated by whatever is in the file he's holding.

She waves a hand. 'Almost never, maybe if there's some political trouble. Then there's the likes of Radu, but he's not really from Bucharest. Only acts like it!'

She scoffs again, and gives him that sheepish look of someone who said something they shouldn't have.

Constantin is scribbling furiously, pretending to be copying from the files. He lets a moment pass, another one.

Then, like a man completely engrossed in his work who's just politely keeping up with conversation, he says, 'Radu?'

'Oh, that mad agitator Mantea's boy. My twins were in the same class but they didn't do nearly as well. Presidential administration!' She rolls her eyes.

He turns to her. 'Comrade Mantea?' he asks.

'He's my friend,' Lia says. 'He lives in the tower block next to ours.'

Comrade Mantea's son smiles. 'Who would have guessed, the old rebel making friends with such a perfect little patriot.'

Lia looks up and searches the sky again.

'Let's practise, then. What will you tell the Dear Leader when you see him?'

Lia thinks, Comrade Mantea would know what to answer. She even turns back to see if Mother and Dad aren't coming out of the Town Hall; she would feel better if they were here.

'I prepared poems and anthems,' she finally says.

He gives her a gentle nudge with his elbow. 'Come on, you can tell me. I know there's something else. I have kids, too.' He leans in to her and whispers, 'Between you and me – everybody hates the anthems.'

'The colours. I want to ask about the colours.'

She tells him the whole speech she had prepared about the missing colours, about how to make more of them, the colour shop if they're too expensive, that they could ask Germany to see how they manage to have so many colours.

Before she has properly finished telling him, Comrade Mantea's son says, 'Hang on!', then brings a hand to his breast pocket and takes out the most beautiful piece of fabric Lia has ever seen. He opens her palm and gives it to her.

She holds it as if it were a baby bird. The fabric is dark red and blue and shiny and soft. She has never seen anything as beautiful as this. It's soft like kitten fur.

'It's silk. It's yours.'

Lia brings it to her face and rubs it against her cheek. 'Is it from Germany?' she asks.

'It doesn't really matter where it's from.'

She opens up the square of fabric – it's the size of a hand-kerchief – and lays it out across her knees. It mirrors the light just like water.

'This business about not having colours, or only dull colours,' he leans in towards her and whispers again, 'that's just for some people. Not for everyone. Those of us who can appreciate colour, who would go to the trouble to make a special backpack and go to special classes for it, we can have all the colours in the rainbow.'

He's watching her as if there's a right and wrong answer to what he said. Lia is not sure she understands.

'What I'm saying is, if a girl is very good and dedicated, she can have all the colours.'

'I want colours for everyone!' Lia says, and she tells him about the trouble with the fish map, and the astronaut. Comrade Mantea's son laughs so much he chokes on the cigarette smoke.

'I'm beginning to see how you're friends with the old man.' He seems pleased.

Lia is dying to tell him about the present. It's a watch or maybe a small cuckoo clock; she could hear the box ticking. But she remembers Comrade Mantea's voice and sees his wide-open eyes, telling her not to mention the present to anyone, *under any circumstances.*

They hear the roar then. The Dear Leader! Lia claps her hands like the people in the street. Comrade Mantea's son musses her hair.

The black thing swoops in over the stadium. The roar dies down. Lia stands up and straightens her uniform. It can't be long now; the people in the street are full of oomph again, chanting and flag-waving.

'Well, here is our Dear Leader,' Comrade Mantea's son says. 'I'm sure you'll make a smashing impression with your poems.'

Lia can't hold it in any more. 'We have a secret present for him as well!' she says and pats the backpack.

Comrade Mantea's son's smile turns into a puzzled frown.

The Mayor rushes up to them then, takes her hand and says, 'Let's go, child. It's time. At long last!'

Constantin is just inside the Town Hall, still out of breath after running there from the archives. He asked for Comrade Presidential Advisor Mantea and a woman pointed at a man sitting outside, on the steps, next to a schoolgirl.

He can only see the man's back.

Constantin's hand is on his service weapon inside his jacket, but he stops himself from rushing out. He can't risk the arrest turning into a hostage situation with a child.

There's a roar then – the presidential helicopter arrives.

Commotion follows; everybody inside the Town Hall hurries out. The girl and the suspect stand up, too. The man appears to be in his thirties or early forties. Tall, athletic.

An older man wearing a tricolour sash over his suit takes the girl by the hand and leads her away.

Constantin runs out. The suspect is still there, his back to Constantin, staring at the child that is being led away. By the time he moves, Constantin's hand is on his shoulder and the barrel of the gun against the man's back.

'You're under arrest,' Constantin says.

The gun is still hidden inside his suit jacket; he's afraid one of the security agents on the rooftops might shoot him if he waves a gun around with the President nearby.

'What?' Radu says.

Constantin pushes his fingers into the man's shoulder, turns him around by force while remaining behind him. 'You're under arrest. We're going to walk together into the Town Hall.'

'Do you even know who I am?'

'Radu Mantea, you are under arrest. Now, just walk,' Constantin says.

The man tries to turn his head.

'You're incredibly close to being shot dead,' Constantin says.

'Can't we do this after the visit? Everybody knows me, it's not like I'm going to disappear. You're some cop, aren't you? The one who stayed at the palace?'

'Go.' Constantin shoves him through the doors. The great hall is completely empty; everyone has left for the parade. Constantin takes his gun out of the jacket and backs away from the killer.

Radu turns around, his hands in the air. Constantin is surprised. The man doesn't look like a savage, compulsive killer. He looks . . . polished. Civilised.

'Dear God!' A woman has just stepped out of a room. From the looks of it she's a cleaner; she's dropped the mop she was holding. She let those words escape her and now she just stands there, covering her mouth with her hand as if to prevent more words from flying out.

'Comrade!' Radu shouts to her. 'You're going to be my witness. There's going to be an attempt on Comrade Ceauşescu's life and this man is trying to stop me from intervening.'

This is probably the most ludicrous and incompetent escape idea that Constantin has ever heard from a suspect.

'Fine,' Constantin says. 'We'll just stand here and wait for the non-attempt to pass.'

But the man doesn't look thwarted, or desperate to convince Constantin. He looks confident.

'The child you saw me speaking to, just now, on the steps, she has a bomb in her backpack.' Radu is speaking calmly, but in a low voice, presumably so the woman doesn't hear. 'I didn't put it there because I'm not an alcoholic fantasist, and she'll never get that past Nicolae's personal security. But the child is meant to travel with him in the parade car. She just told me someone gave her a secret present for the Dear Leader to put in her backpack. I know that person, he's my father. I know he hates Ceaușescu. I know he can make a bomb. That child has a bomb.'

Constantin shakes his head, laughs. 'You really are crazy,' he says. But something nags at him. Something in Radu's story rings a bell.

Radu turns to the woman. 'You'll remember what I told you, yes? When everyone will come looking for the traitor. I tried to intervene.'

'There's no bomb, Comrade!' Constantin shouts to the woman. 'I'm a police officer. This man is under arrest. You can go back to what you were doing.'

Radu smiles. He does something with his right hand. Constantin realises he's holding up two fingers.

Constantin suddenly remembers the archivist's words. *That crazy agitator Mantea.*

'Two little dead girls,' Radu says.

The Mayor's hand is sweaty but Lia doesn't let go. As they reach the bottom of the steps, she gets a good look at the military band waiting for the parade to start. The uniforms with golden braids, the brass trumpets! The flags, the flowers, the balloons! There's so much colour today.

At street level now, he pulls her through the throng with the help of two men who are pressing ahead and shouting 'Officials! Officials!' Then they are at the barrier by the car park.

She spots Mother and Dad. They are watching her from across the car park by the fence.

'He came!' Lia shouts. 'I'm going in the car!'

Dad waves, but Mother puts her finger in front of her lips. She doesn't like Lia to shout.

A soldier comes up to her and the Mayor. 'Our permits, here,' he says to the soldier.

'There he is!' Lia forgets herself and shouts again. Comrade Mantea is at the opposite corner, just outside the fence of the parking area. He is looking at the open-top car that she and the Dear Leader will ride in. She waves to him. He doesn't see her. Then someone moves away from the fence and Lia sees that Comrade Mantea's arm is in a big plaster cast. What could possibly have happened? He was fine just yesterday afternoon.

The barrier lifts then, and the Mayor pulls her through.

They go towards the open-top car that's parked at the back. The Dear Leader has just arrived, too. He looks a lot older than on TV. She's pretty sure she's not allowed to say that to him.

A man who's by the car puts up his hand towards the Mayor and says, 'Wait there.'

They stop. The Mayor doesn't let go of her hand.

Lia turns around to see if Comrade Mantea is following them, but he's not in the car park and she can no longer see him by the fence either.

They just stand there, in the sun. Beyond the back fence there's a tree with yellowish catkins; they could have let them wait there, in the shade. Her tummy hurts again. Her feet; she's been waiting on those steps forever. What was the point of making her practise all that standing up straight and being cheerful when the Dear Leader is so late for the meeting that she needs a nap?

'The sweets!' she suddenly says out loud, startling the Mayor.

She mustn't forget to tell the Dear Leader to start making some nice sweets. The ones she buys from the local shop are lumps of hard, sticky, see-through sugar which everyone ends up eating with the fluff from the paper bags they're sold in. But once, a guest of Mother's brought a little plastic pouch full of glossy jellybeans. They tasted glossy, too. 'For the children. From Germany,' the woman had said. Orange, green, yellow, red – those jellybeans had incredible colours. And no paper fluff.

There's a loud noise then, like a bang, and everyone turns towards the Town Hall. The men in suits surround the car with the President. They all have guns.

'It'll be some kid with firecrackers,' one of the men says.

'I'll send someone to check,' another man says, and talks into a radio.

They put their guns down.

The flag-waving picks up again.

Constantin runs down the Town Hall steps and to the car park. Everything seems normal: music, crowd, chanting. The military band is lined up on the road, waiting for the start of the parade.

He wonders if he's lost his mind.

He pushes people aside, runs to the car park barrier, sees the open-top car at the back, sees Ceauşescu and five security men. The girl is standing with the Mayor some five metres away.

He will just go and take the girl's backpack. If it turns out it was nothing, he will explain later.

Constantin shoves his badge in front of a soldier guarding the barrier, demanding to be let through.

251

They let him pass.

He mustn't run now. They will shoot him if he runs at the car. He walks with his hands held high and the badge in one of them, eyes locked on the girl; he wills her not to move. If someone is detonating the bomb remotely, they will wait until she gets closer to Ceaușescu.

He has almost reached the girl when there is sudden shouting. Everyone turns towards a heavily armed soldier approaching the presidential car together with an old man who has a cast on his right arm. The soldier is pointing his gun at the old man.

Ceaușescu's security team shout 'Stop!' and point their guns at the two men. The soldier obeys. He shouts, 'This citizen here says there's a bomb in that child's backpack! That he saw someone here give it to her. Swears on it.'

He shrugs and keeps pointing the gun at the old man.

Everybody turns to the girl. Constantin raises his hands, shouts so they can hear him by the car, 'I think it's true! We received the same information.'

The Mayor backs away from the girl with quick steps.

The child looks afraid.

Constantin is finally by her side. He recognises her – it's the kid he talked to the last time he was here. He's briefly taken aback by the coincidence. But there's no time: he would like to be gentle, explain, but instead he tears the backpack off her and then throws it as far as he can beyond the fence of the car park, down on to the riverbank. Everybody ducks instinctively.

There's no explosion.

Constantin turns towards the open-top car. For some reason, the old man with the cast is running towards it, he's almost by the car. Ceauşescu's bodyguards have just recovered from the suspense of waiting for an explosion and are a fraction of a second from noticing him. The soldier, also waiting for an explosion, hasn't noticed that he's lost his man.

Constantin has a black feeling about what is going on before he actually formulates the thought. He throws himself to the ground, pulls the child down with him.

13

Pitești, August

'It's like the moon landing,' the girl's father whispers to Constantin. 'Do you remember? The whole country huddled together around the radio.'

Constantin is on the sofa in his living room. Sandu is on his lap, playing with a Rubik cube. The child, Lia, and her parents, Victor and Silvia, are staying with them tonight. Maybe longer, depending on what the hell is going to happen. Nobody seems to be fully in charge any more. Securitate wanted everyone in the car park arrested and sent to Bucharest, but when Constantin said that he knows the family, that the child was a potential victim in the attack, and that the family will stay with him and be available to the investigation if needed, they relented.

Constantin checks his watch. Half an hour until the news. Is he dead? Is he not dead? Will they tell us either way?

The girl is over in the armchair. She's been very quiet, and he hasn't found a moment to talk to her alone. Tina and Silvia are in the kitchen, improvising something to eat. Constantin tries to gently shift Sandu in his arms so he can get the weight off his left buttock. He has a few shrapnel cuts in his lower back and buttocks, nothing serious. Most of the blast probably went into the bodyguards. The girl doesn't have a single scratch.

Ceauşescu, gone: he can hardly imagine it. He wishes now he had turned back to see what happened to the people by the car, but he didn't know whether there was going to be another explosion, so he just grabbed the girl and ran.

The phone rings.

Constantin offloads Sandu on the sofa and goes to the hallway.

'Guess the damn weapon,' Davidescu says by way of hello.

Earlier today, right after the blast, it had taken all of Constantin's persuasive powers to get Davidescu to go to Radu's home and secure any possible evidence. The man didn't really want to search the home of a presidential advisor, not even now. What convinced him was the argument that, politically, things might change, and it won't look great that the police paraded a bear as a serial killer. The police will need to prove that the killer was a high-ranking official and the disinformation was orchestrated from higher up.

'You found it? That's fantastic. Titus thought it was some kind of grappling hook,' Constantin says.

'Baldy is an amateur. A scimitar! A goddamn museum artefact.'

'Huh,' Constantin says. Now that's a word straight out of the history books. 'You'll keep it safe, yes? We don't want it to somehow disappear.'

'I don't need you to tell me how to do my fucking job.'

'I know, I'm just . . . Was there anything else?'

'Copies of informers' notes. A bunch of letters to his father that he never sent. Full of shit.'

'Incriminating shit?'

'Did it to prove to his old man that he was not some regime stooge.'

'Christ. But that's all we need, then,' Constantin says. He feels elated that Davidescu found solid evidence. It occurs to him then that Davidescu will probably take the credit for stopping the bear. Constantin realises he's fine with it. He double-checks – yes, it's absolutely fine.

Lia stands up from the sofa. She feels strange. Something is different, some big thing that changes everything, like the weather, but not really the weather.

'Where are you going?' Dad asks.

'Bathroom,' Lia says, and then she goes out of the room, past the bathroom, past the kitchen, and into the long hallway where the nice policeman is talking on the phone.

'Christ. But that's all we need, then,' the policeman says into the phone.

He sees Lia. 'All right. I'll be in the office tomorrow.'

He hangs up.

'Hello,' he says.

Lia puts her finger to her lips to make him talk quieter. 'Where's Comrade Mantea?' she whispers.

She did not see him again after the blast at the car park, and she's afraid to ask Mother and Dad about him. But the last time she saw him, when he was with that soldier, he was as far from the exploding car as she was. He will be fine. Except for his broken arm.

The policeman looks confused for a moment. Then he says, 'Ah, you mean . . . the old man.'

'He's my friend. Mother and Dad don't like him.'

The man runs his hand through his hair. The back of his hand is full of scratches and cuts from the bomb. He looks like he, too, tried to wash an orange cat.

'I'll find out. But can you tell me something?' He crouches so he is as tall as her. 'Why was there a clock in your backpack?' He is whispering.

Lia tells him about the present and the colours. Without meaning to, she starts crying. It was supposed to be nice, everything like at the end of a really nice fairy tale. But nothing happened the way it was supposed to. She didn't speak to the Dear Leader about the colours, Comrade Mantea was strange, they had an explosion, and now they are in this strange house.

'It was a nice plan,' the policeman says, which just makes her cry more. 'But I wouldn't tell anyone. Hey, listen to me. I took the backpack from the riverbank. Nobody else knows about the clock. It's best this way. All right?'

They go back to the living room. Constantin steals a glance at the girl's father: the man seems exhausted. The woman was even worse; she was in shock when she ran up to him and the girl after the blast. Everyone's had quite a day.

He already knows he will spend a lot of time thinking about the old man with the cast. What was the plan, was that really it – to use the warning about the ticking 'bomb' in the girl's backpack to get close enough to Ceaușescu? It's insane that it worked. Or, almost. They will find out soon.

One old man had more courage than twenty million people, including youngish policemen who would have been better placed to try to right the universe.

But did Mantea know about his son? Was this some kind of crazy dare between father and son?

'To new beginnings!' Victor raises his glass. Constantin picks up his glass and toasts.

They hear music then from the kitchen. It's some kind of Latin-American dance song. Constantin waits: any second now Tina will turn it off. But no. There's laughter from the kitchen. Constantin can't believe it.

The women come in with small plates, cutlery and a tray of nibbles – biscuits, a few shrivelled olives and slices of yellow cheese. There's booze, too; the sparkling water bottle full of plum brandy that Tina's father sends every year.

They help themselves from the tray.

The phone rings again. Constantin hobbles to the hallway; his leg fell asleep under Sandu's weight.

'So you fought a bear and won,' Titus says.

'I did no such thing. I shot an unarmed man in the leg like a proper coward.'

'Really?'

'Titus, give me a break. How are you feeling?'

'There's a rumour. A very serious rumour. About what happened in this town you just visited.'

Constantin does the usual check in his head: what's OK to say over the phone, what isn't.

'The rumour is true,' he says.

'He's dead?' Titus asks.

'I don't know. But it's possible.'

Silence at the other end. Then, 'I heard a new joke.'

Constantin doesn't know what to say, so he shrugs.

'A new convict arrives at the prison,' Titus says. 'His cell-mates ask him the usual question – *so, what brings you here? Laziness, our guy says. Laziness brought me here.* The other prisoners are surprised. Shocked, even. *Laziness, really? They're locking us up for being lazy now?'*

A frisson courses through Constantin. It's absolutely not the kind of joke they should be saying over the phone. 'Titus . . .'

'Well, it's like this, our guy says. One evening I had drinks and a chat with a friend, and you know how it is, over a drink everyone says something they shouldn't have said. I thought to myself, I'll take it easy tonight but first thing tomorrow I'll go to Securitate to let them know what he said. But what do you know – my diligent friend went to see them the same evening.'

They are both quiet. Constantin's heart is racing. He thought they would be cut off.

'You're still there?' Titus asks.

'Yeah.'

'Hm. Maybe he really is dead,' Titus says and hangs up.

Constantin returns to the living room a little dazed. *Maybe he really is dead.* The enormity of it.

'Please, have some more,' Tina pushes the tray closer to Victor and Silvia.

Constantin hasn't told Tina everything, just that this family will be spending the evening with them. That they're good people. She didn't protest.

He sits back down. Sandu's one sock slips off. The summery music is still playing in the kitchen. The olives are are on the salty side but with the cheese they're just right.

'Two minutes left,' Dad says.

Mother's hand is still trembling a little, and now and again she puts her arm around Lia and squeezes her tight. The whole afternoon Mother kept repeating that the minutes between the blast and when she finally saw that Lia was fine were the worst of her life. She had looked mad when she ran up to Lia.

Lia remembers the handkerchief. It's hidden in the front pocket of the parade dress. It's so beautiful that anyone who sees it will surely try to steal it. She will keep the handkerchief forever, not show it to anyone except for Comrade Mantea. She can picture the scene: they will be in his kitchen, and she will unfold the handkerchief on the table like a magician. He'll pretend to take it to blow his nose in it, and she will snatch it back, then they will both laugh one of their best-ever belly laughs.

'Could it really be that he's gone?' Mother whispers to herself. She's looking at the TV.

The news is about to start.

ACKNOWLEDGEMENTS

I would like to thank early *Astronaut!* readers Laura Beatty, Toby Follett, Vicky Grut, Josef Hedlund and Annemarie Neary for their feedback, my writing group friends Anne Aylor, Rob Carroll, Gavin Eyers, Roger Levy and Elise Valmorbida, and Stephanie Brann, Nash Colundalur, Tania Dain, Adam Lafene, Leonie Milliner and Lucy Smith, my agent Sophie Scard for her support, and my editor Ella Gordon for believing in the novel and helping make it better.

RAISING READERS
Books Build Bright Futures

Dear Reader,

We'd love your attention for one more page to tell you about the crisis in children's reading, and what we can all do.

Studies have shown that reading for fun is the **single biggest predictor of a child's future success** – more than family circumstance, parents' educational background or income. It improves academic results, mental health, wealth, communication skills and ambition.

The number of children reading for fun is in rapid decline. Young people have a lot of competition for their time, and a worryingly high number do not have a single book at home.

Our business works extensively with schools, libraries and literacy charities, but here are some ways we can all raise more readers:

- Reading to children for just 10 minutes a day makes a difference
- Don't give up if children aren't regular readers – there will be books for them!
- Visit bookshops and libraries to get recommendations
- Encourage them to listen to audiobooks
- Support school libraries
- Give books as gifts

Thank you for reading: there's a lot more information about how to encourage children to read on our website.

www.JoinRaisingReaders.com